Also from Indigo Sea Press
Novels by Carol Pearce Bjorlie

Sweet Harmony
Life in Harmony

indigoseapress.com

Perfect Harmony

By

Carol Pearce Bjorlie

Sepia Books
Published by Indigo Sea Press
Winston-Salem

Sepia Books
Indigo Sea Press
302 Ricks Drive
Winston-Salem, NC 27103

First Sepia Books edition published
January, 2016
Sepia Books, Moon Sailor and all production design are trademarks of Indigo Sea Press, used under license.

For information regarding bulk purchases of this book, digital purchase and special discounts, please contact the publisher at indigoseapress.com

Cover design by Stacy Castanedo

Manufactured in the United States of America
ISBN 978-1-63066-210-3

For the Burmeister and Brenna families

SEPTEMBER, 1938

Iris stood in the doorway yawning. Her father sat at the kitchen table, a pot of coffee in front of him. "What's for breakfast?" she asked.

"Whatever you make," he replied.

Her mother came into the room, wandered over to the rocker by the fireplace, and dumped herself into the chair. Her husband limped to her side, his cane in one hand and a soda cracker in the other. He still had a bandage on the back of his head. It was going to hurt when he took it off. His hair had begun to grow underneath it. He fanned his wife's pink face with his hand.

"Horace, stop." Laura Ellen's face paled and she jumped from the chair and ran to the bathroom.

Horace held the cracker towards Cookie. The black lab was on her feet in an instant. The cracker disappeared.

"You didn't see that, did you, Iris?" her father asked.

"I did, but I'm not telling." She hollered up the stairs, "Merry, speed it up! I want to be early on the first day."

"Coming, coming," her sister yelled back.

Her father asked, "Iris, could you keep the noise down?" He slumped into a chair. His head wound and broken leg, healing from his fall at Niagara Cave two months ago, still gave him pain. "Where's your little sister?"

"She's pretending she's going to school too. She's getting dressed. You should see her. She put her Sunday dress on over her pajama bottoms. She has on my Sunday hat, the one with pink ribbons. What will she do when she really goes to school?" Iris took an apple from the bowl on the table, cut it in half, and took a big chunk in her mouth.

"I'm going to fix a tomato sandwich for my lunch like I used to do at home," said Iris. Then she thought, oh, I am home.

Her father asked, "Don't you want a slice of ham with that?"

Merry walked into the kitchen with a book balanced on her

1

head. "Is half that apple for me," she inquired as she picked it up and finished it off.

"Merry! If you wouldn't try to be so perfect you'd be on time," said Iris. "I'm going to school and I'm leaving right now."

"What about breakfast? Where's Mother?" Merry asked.

Iris nodded towards the bathroom. "In there again."

"Yuck," said Merry. "I'm not having babies, oh, no. Not ever!"

"Yes, well, I know," said her father. "I also know that neither of you is leaving here without toast and cheese at least." He looked up as his wife came in the kitchen. He brought a cool wash cloth to her but as soon as he came near her she rushed away.

The eighth grade at Harmony School had the fewest number of students in any class. Several boys dropped out and two families moved away. Julie, Iris' best friend told her, "No one ever moves to Harmony—except you." She continued, "Imagine moving to Harmony!" Then she laughed.

In August, Iris and Julie had gotten a letter from their eighth grade teacher, Miss Vollum. She wrote about how much she looked forward to the beginning of school and meeting her new class. She said that for her every year was the best year. Oscar told stories about how strict she was. Miss Vollum believed in homework. She had gray curly hair and was old. She wore funny shoes. Her favorite subject was History and Geography. Each year she had students do projects and write papers on a place on the globe that most interested them. Iris chose Egypt. She wasn't sure why, just that pyramids and mummies seemed like something she'd like to learn about. Also, there was the Bible story about Moses and the Egyptian princess who saved his life. Julie chose Norway for her project. Oscar had done his on Spain.

Iris missed her friend, Oscar Runs Like Fox, on the first day. Oscar moved to the tenth grade which meant he would ride a bus all the way to Bemidji High School. No more riding his pony. It was school bus time for Oscar. The hallways at Iris' school were full of boys and girls in new shoes and ironed shirts and blouses, but there was no shining black head and blue eyes in the crowd. Most of the reservation children attended the Episcopal school for Indians where they boarded all year but Oscar's mother had insisted he attend Harmony Elementary where she had taught.

For her Egyptian project, Iris talked her father into helping her construct a pyramid. She wasn't sure how it would turn out but she wanted there to be steps which she would paint to look like stone. The pyramid would sit on a flat base. When you picked it up, a mummy, fake jewels, and gold would be underneath.

Iris went to the school library after class on Friday and sat at a long table in the back of the big room with The Encyclopedia Britannica, Volume E, Earth—the Everglades, in front of her. She didn't want to be disturbed. Her project would be the best Miss Vollum had ever read. "Egypt" came after "Eggs" in the Encyclopedia. She would draw a map of Egypt. Her teacher liked maps. Iris thought she'd do one in color, making tiny waves on the Nile in green and blue. Egypt was so old that Iris' mind went blank trying to imagine it. Who could even think about 3100 BC? She flipped through pages and pages of tiny print about Paleolithic climate, Imhotep's priestly titles, "Great Seer, Physician, Thinker, Architect," Ah! Architect. The first step pyramids. Iris yawned and read: "Achievements in mighty constructions during the reign of the fourth dynasty…"

Iris rested her head on her arms. Behind her closed eyelids she saw people marching: dark people with long black hair, men with wolf heads, men with eagles on their shoulders. They walked in single file down a dark tunnel. The only light was from the shining walls. There she was, Iris Anderson, being led into the deepest chamber of a crypt. The floor was yellow brick and the room cylindrical. In one second the marching Egyptians disappeared, and there she was in the glowing pit

3

alone. There were no doors but she saw a ledge high over her head. Something was seated on it, something inhuman. She turned around. There was a sharp-beaked eagle on another ledge. Large shelves began to slide out of the wall, one held a coiled cobra, head flared, tongue flicking, and another presented a scorpion the size of her father's shoes, tail raised. She heard a growl and more doors opened. Tigers walked into her enclosure padding on their huge paws, eyes mere slits. Her heart beat so loud it sounded like a drum. She realized the big cats were pacing around her in a circle, close, closer. Her heart raced. "Boom!" The sound of ledges pulling into the wall allowing all the creatures to fall to the floor around her was deafening. The cobra, scorpion, eagle and tigers were all on her level. Where could she go? "Boom!" "Boom!" Iris opened her eyes. It was dark. She was in the library. She closed the book where her head had rested. "Boom," a sound exploded in the room. Iris jumped out of her chair. She looked at the windows, ones replaced after last year's tornado. There was a blinding fork of light in the purple sky followed by a "Ca-ra-a-a-k!" of thunder. In the next flash of lightning she saw that the clock read 5:00.

She had slept for an hour and a half! The librarians had turned out the lights. Everyone had gone home. How had the librarian missed her? She ran to the library door and screamed. Lightning revealed the school's mascot, a golden eagle perched on a pedestal by the librarian's desk. Iris was certain she'd seen the wings move. The doors to the hallway were locked. She pulled and wrestled with the glass doorknobs. There were two small windows above the doors which opened to let in fresh air. They were open now. She pulled a library table to the door. If she stood on it she could just reach the window. From here she could see out the front door of the school, cornfields waving in the violent wind, rain pelting the windows. Didn't her mother wonder where she was? She told her mother she would stay to work in the library after school. Someone must be outside. Merry had gone home with a friend. Maybe her parents called the principal. The sky was turning green. Didn't the sky turn

4

green before a tornado? She got a chair and sat it on the library table. She threw one leg over the opening in the small window. She could just fit through. She pushed the other leg over the ledge and hung by her fingers from the window frame. It was sharp. Then she dropped. She landed on her hands and knees and ran for the front door as she saw a dark figure appear and smash the window glass. Iris screamed until she heard a voice, "Iris! Iris!" The door opened and Iris flew into Earl Runs Like Fox's arms. Oscar stood behind him grinning.

"Iris," he said, "you sure love school!"

That's when Iris noticed a sharp pain in her right hand. She looked at it in the dim light. Her pinkie was bent and bleeding. One knee had a deep scrape.

Iris' father couldn't drive with a broken leg. Her mother had called Earl Runs Like Fox and asked him to go to the school and see if he could find her daughter. In an earlier call the principal had assured her that all the children were out of the building. Earl and Oscar delivered Iris home teary; holding her right hand up in the air. Her mother drove her to see Dr. Brenna. Not only was her finger broken, there was a cut down to the bone on the back of it. Dr. Brenna cleaned her finger and knee and bandaged them. Iris held her mother's hand and didn't cry. Next he broke a wooden tongue depressor in half and taped it to hold the swollen finger straight. He looked at Iris and said, "All right now. I do not want to see another Anderson in my office until that baby comes. You girls stay out of the way of roosters, barn posts, caves, and don't climb any more library walls, you hear?" Then he winked at Iris and dug a sucker out of his deep white coat pocket. He also handed one to Iris' mother. "Here, you probably need this more than your daughter," he said. "You've got your hands full with these girls!"

On the way home, Iris told her mother about her dream. "Mother, do I have to do my project on Egypt? Couldn't I choose Norway or some calm place?"

Her mother laughed, "Norway? Calm? Why Iris, those

Vikings used to wrestle trees!"
Iris laughed with her, "Trees?"

Iris stayed home from school. She kept close to her mother
in the kitchen and held her hand up in the air to keep the
swelling down. Her knee throbbed. It was her right hand, so she
couldn't write or eat without bumping it. It hurt. She picked up
the milk pitcher once, bumped her finger and dropped the milk.
Her finger seemed to holler out to her and hurt so bad she felt
weak-kneed, sat down, and cried. Her father found her like that.
He used a cane at home and couldn't lean over because of his
head injury. "Ah, Iris, this won't do. Your mother's lying
down, I can't bend over, and you've got a broken finger." He
called up the stairs, "Martha Rose, we need you."

Martha Rose clumped down the stairs in a pair of old boots.
"Wha' cha' want, Daddy?" she asked.

"Would you please take a cloth and swipe up this milk?"

"Swipe?" repeated the little girl.

"You know, clean it up," her father said.

"I don't know if I can. I'm still hurt bad," said the little girl,
as she to limped to the sink.

In the afternoon, Iris lay down on the sofa and fell asleep.
Both kittens, Muffin and Biscuit, settled next to her. How could
one broken finger make her whole body feel bad? As soon as
the dream started she tried to wake up, but couldn't. Her
eyelids were heavy. She fretted and tried to call out but her lips
were sealed. She was in the pit right where she left off her
dream in the library. A ledge shot out to her about knee height
and she leaped on it out of reach of the snake, scorpion and dog
with a wolf's head. Another shelf appeared and she climbed
onto it. All the creatures were trying to get to her. Tigers began
to climb after her but the ledges below her slid back into the
wall. She climbed higher as ledges appeared. Suddenly she
heard more wings. It was the gold eagle from the library! It
dived towards her and when she looked up she saw light at the
top of her cylindrical prison. She protected her face with her

6

arms, "Go away," she screamed. "Go away!"

"Iris, Iris, wake up, Honey," her mother said.

Iris' eyes opened and there sat her mother next to her on the sofa.

"Bad dream again?" she asked.

Iris grabbed her mother. "The worst! It was the dream I had in the library only worse. Is this going to happen every time I fall asleep?"

"No, I'm sure it won't," answered her mother. "You had a shock yesterday. Why don't you sit in the sun? Enjoy this beautiful day. Martha Rose has her dolls outside and after yesterday's storm it's pleasant today."

Iris followed her mother's advice. She found Martha Rose by the garden. She had her dolls under the shade of a gigantic rhubarb plant. Leaves and small limbs blown about by the storm covered the ground.

Martha Rose looked up as her big sister came out of the house. "Look at these big leafs. They're roofs for my dolls. Here, Samantha can be your baby today."

Iris lay down on her stomach in the sun. "I don't feel like being Samantha's mother," she said. She laid still and listened to her sister prattle to her dolls. Her mother came outside with a chair and her knitting and sat under an apple tree. All the leaves hadn't blown away and the shade was nice. She rested her knitting on her growing tummy.

Iris thought, this is what it's like to be home all day, Martha Rose takes care of her doll family, her mother knits, father reads a book in the living room with his leg propped on a chair. All the time Iris and Merry were at school life went on at the farm. No wonder Martha Rose is happy.

Oscar rode over after school. He stayed so late that her mother invited him for dinner. He said, "Yes!" He inspected Iris' splint. "You're lucky that's all you broke," he said.

After dinner she walked outside with him to his pony tied up at the barn. "I don't mean this in a bad way but Iris, you don't look right," he said.

"I don't feel right," she answered. "I feel, oh, I don't know, scared, or something." She told him about her dreams. "I'm afraid to go to sleep tonight," she confided. "I don't want to have that dream ever again." She could feel the sting of tears threaten.

Her friend tipped his head to one side, and suggested, "Before you go to bed tonight, turn your pillow over."

"That's not going to help this nightmare."

"Turn your pillow over. Try it," Oscar said. "It's what my mother had me do when I had nightmares. It worked." Blue was in a stall between Joshua and War Bonnet. The horses seemed to have a language of nickers and snorts. Oscar put one foot on a stall slat and jumped up on Blue's back. "Remember what I told you. Turn your pillow over. Punch it for good luck."

Iris waved goodbye from the barn door.

That night Iris wore her blue nightgown with yellow and white daisies around the neck. She slid between her sheets, turned her pillow over once, punched it, closed her eyes and fell asleep. She woke to the sound of chickens clucking. There was a woman sitting in her chair, a stranger Iris could see through. The woman had golden braids twirled into a crown on her head and blue eyes like Oscar's. When Iris sat up, the woman smiled and then her image grew dim. The last Iris saw of her was a gleam of blonde hair. She knew who it was. She'd seen her picture at Oscar's house. Iris threw back her covers and smiled. Oscar was right, no dreams.

OCTOBER

Iris looked forward to a morning when her mother would not run to the bathroom when coffee perked. (The smell of it made her sick.) Iris' father offered to give coffee up for the duration of her mother's pregnancy but she wouldn't let him do that.

Iris' father walked without his cane, limping, but on his own. The cast still slowed him down, and he stumped and clumped about the house. His leg was taking a long time to heal. It itched under the cast, and he knocked against the hard plaster, and stuck his wife's knitting needles down to scratch it. Martha Rose's ankle healed quickly, but she talked about it like it happened yesterday, not last July.

The October sky was the deep blue of bachelor button flowers that bloomed in July. Iris could not stay indoors. The wind was clean and sweet. Birch leaves were yellow as canaries. October was Iris' favorite month of the year, especially in Virginia. The maple trees on Brook Road turned vibrant red. The cemetery at Emmanuel Episcopal church was covered with crepe myrtle leaves but the magnolias stayed green and magnificent. Iris knew what was coming soon for Harmony—snow, and inevitable white. When she got tired of white there would be white. She did love this blue October sky, though. She stared at it and listened to the cacophony of migrating geese.

She had on a scratchy wool sweater, the first time she'd worn one this year. She sat down to keep her promise to her mother to write her Uncle Luke and invite him for Thanksgiving. The little Iris knew about her Uncle Luke was that he was her father's only brother and younger than her Dad. He taught at a college in Northern Minnesota and wrote poetry. She met him in Virginia when she was five years old, but all she remembered about him was that he sang. She wanted to be a poet too, and hoped he could tell her how to do it. Her letter began:

9

Dear Uncle Luke,

This is Iris, your niece. I am thirteen and in the eighth grade. I'm learning about Egypt, the pyramids, and mummies for my History class. I always get good grades.

You will be glad to hear that after his fall in the cave three months ago, Daddy can walk without his cane or crutches, and will have his cast off when you see him at Thanksgiving. That means you will not get to see him hop about on one foot. I can hardly believe you are really coming to Harmony. It's so small that if you blink, you will miss it, but you know that.

I wonder if you can tell me how to get to be a poet, because I want to be one. I like to read John Greenleaf Whittier. His poems are in a book you left here a long time ago.

Love, Iris,
Your Niece

Iris gave the letter to her mother to read. Her mother folded it and put it in the envelope with her invitation to Luke to come for Thanksgiving Holidays. "Iris," she said, "you've got one lucky uncle. I hope you become good friends."

Sure enough, two weeks later Iris pulled a long white envelope out of the mailbox. It was addressed to "Miss Iris Andersen." She ran into the house with it. "Mother, Daddy," she called. "Uncle Luke wrote me back!" She could hardly tear the envelope open fast enough. She read out loud.

Dear Niece,

I am coming to Sweet Harmony! You and I can read all the John Greenleaf Whittier you want. I especially love his poem, "Snowbound," how about you? I can't believe your family has been on the farm for over a year, and I haven't visited.

I will bring a BIG surprise! Can't wait to see you all.

Love,
Uncle Luke

Iris turned to her mother, "He likes 'Snowbound!' Can you believe that? Oh, I hope it does snow, and we can read it in front of the fire like last year and Laughing Sky can come, and Oscar and his Daddy. Oh! He's really coming. Wait 'till he meets Martha Rose!"

Iris read and re-read the letter. Why didn't he say exactly when he'd arrive and what BIG surprise?

Iris' project on Egypt got an "A+". She and her father worked on the wooden pyramid after school in the barn by kerosene lantern for two weeks. It was a hit with her class. When you picked up the top of the pyramid there were tiny pieces of cloth wrapped around sticks which were the mummies, and she had painted small stones yellow and placed them around like gold. She drew a map of Egypt on a sheet of drawing paper from school, and then her mother burned the edges with a match so it looked ancient. She even changed her handwriting to look old and spidery.

She didn't tell anyone about her dream but she knew she would never forget it, even when she was an old woman. The silo on the farm reminded her of the yellow brick cylinder where she had been trapped. She wouldn't go in it for anything. She would also remember the pale figure of the smiling woman with blonde braids who sat in her chair when she woke.

Her mother's stomach began to grow. Thinking of a baby in there was impossible. Iris would be fourteen this month. Fourteen years ago she was "in there." How had she breathed? Maybe there'd be another sister. Of course, Martha Rose was already calling it Benjamin. She liked to lean next to her mother and whisper over the bulge, "Hello, Benjamin. It's Martha Rose, your big sister. Remember me?"

Iris was surprised how firm her mother's bulge became.

Iris helped her father bring a cradle down from the attic. He sat it on the kitchen table for inspection. Her mother said, "Think of the babies who have slept here."

"And cried here and wet here," continued her husband. "It needs a good polish."

Merry asked, "Why'd you bring that thing down? Nobody

needs it, yet!"

"Oh, don't be cross, Merry," said her mother. "I need to believe something is going to come of all those awful mornings." She talked to her tummy. "Sleep well little one, soon you'll be the star of the show."

"And Martha Rose will take a back seat," added Merry.

"I don't think that will happen," replied her father. "It will take a lot to upstage Martha Rose."

Cookie walked over to see what everyone's attention was drawn to, sniffed the cradle, and sneezed.

"What are you going to think of a baby, huh, Cookie?" asked Merry.

Cookie turned her moss brown eyes to Merry and her ears perked up at her name.

Merry asked, "Mother, don't you wish dogs could talk?"

"No," replied her mother. "We have all the talkers we need here. That's one thing I love about Cookie, I can talk to her but she can't talk back."

Laura Ellen turned to her husband, "Speaking of dogs, Horace, where is that dog that howls at night? At least Cookie doesn't howl. Someone on a farm near us must have a new hound dog. It kept me up last night. Did anyone else hear it?"

"That wasn't a dog, sweet wife."

"What could howl like that if it wasn't a hound dog?"

"A wolf," said her husband. "I better check the chicken house."

"Let me come, Daddy," said Iris, reaching for her coat.

"It might not be a pretty sight but come on. I wasn't a high school teacher for nothing. There's lessons to learn on a farm, too."

Iris followed her father to the hutch behind the barn. She knew the news wasn't pretty when she saw hen feathers scattered on the ground before they turned the corner of the barn.

"Dad-burn-it!" said Horace. "That wolf tore the door open and helped himself."

Two hens were gone. Thumbelina was a tumble of bloody

feathers. She lay on her back with her feet in the air.

"Daddy, we can't let Merry or Martha Rose see this. We should bury her."

"Yes, Sweetheart. I'll get her and you get a shovel."

"After that, how do we keep the wolf out?"

"We kill it," said her father. "I'll stay out tonight and get that monster."

"Oh, Daddy, do you have to shoot it?"

"Suppose it was Cookie. Suppose the wolf gets in the barn? I'm afraid it's all I can do. Life and death, death and life, that's a farm. I'm sorry you had to see this, Iris."

"Oh, Daddy, do you have to shoot it?" Iris said again quietly. She brought the shovel for her father and he began to dig a hole behind the barn.

On the twenty-fourth, Iris woke to find a large package on the chair next to her bed. It was at least three feet tall and two feet wide. It was wrapped in brown paper. She jumped out of bed and tore the paper off. Her grandmother had sent Iris her prized possession! The heavy gold frame was the same: the same chinks and dull finish. Queen Guinevere hadn't moved. She stood next to a castle and looked over her shoulder at The Black Knight. The breeze of horses passing made folds in her velvet gown brush against her legs. The blue cape still clung to her shoulders. Her ladies-in-waiting stood behind her talking behind their hands. This oil painting was over a hundred years old. No one knew who painted it, or how the family came to own it. It had always hung over her grandmother's fireplace. Now, it was in Iris' room. She picked it up. It was heavy. She put it in her chair again, and looked around her room. She needed to find a spot where she could see it from her bed. It also needed to hang out of direct sunlight. She sat on her bed. There, between the two windows on the side of the house. That's where Guinevere would be. This was the best birthday gift ever!

Two nights later Iris woke to the sound of a shot-gun blast. Then another.

She wanted to run downstairs and out the back door. Instead, she cradled her head in her arms and cried. Wolves were big dogs. They were beautiful. It says in the Ten Commandments, "Thou shalt not kill." And her father had purposely killed. Supposed they could have tamed the wolf with food and water. It wouldn't have to eat the chickens then.

At the breakfast table the next morning she gave her father a hard look.

He returned her look with a serious one of his own. "Iris, I killed two wolves last night. There is a pack of them causing destruction on several farms. Laughing Sky heard them sniffing on her porch." He turned to his wife. "Keep Cookie indoors unless she's in the barn." He finished his oatmeal, put his coat on, and picked up the shot-gun from the rack by the back door.

Her mother sat back in her chair, her hand rubbing her stomach. "Your father, Earl, and some other farmers are going out shooting today. I want you all at home."

Iris left her place, took her oatmeal bowl to the sink, and brushed tears from her eyes. "I didn't know being a farmer meant being a killer!"

Her mother began, "Oh, Iris…"

Iris stomped up the stairs.

Here she was on a Saturday morning stuck indoors so people could kill wolves.

It wasn't snowing and not too cold. She had to get out of the house. She hurried down the stairs, put on her coat and mittens, and said, "I'm going out to the barn," in her meanest voice.

Her mother called from the living room, "Take Cookie to visit Joshua!"

Iris called Cookie who jumped up from her warm bed frisky and ready to go. Iris looked at her. "Cookie, how can you be happy all the time?" she asked.

It was chillier than Iris had thought. She ran to the barn, opened one of the big doors a crack, and she and Cookie went in. Joshua was in his stall eating hay and shuffling his feet. Iris went in next to him, got his brush, and began rubbing his glossy neck talking to her big friend. "Joshua, you have the nicest brown coat. You're a good horse, yes you are. You always like me. You never talk back." Cookie pranced around the big hooves. "Cookie, be careful. Don't tease this big guy."

Iris couldn't put Cookie in the stall with War Bonnet. War Bonnet didn't have the patience old Joshua did. War Bonnet looked sleepy. Iris would brush her next.

Cookie began to growl. Iris looked down at the puppy. "There's no need for that noise."

Joshua began to buck his stall. His eyes were wide and a line of hair stood up on his back. Two stalls away War Bonnet whinnied, her eyes wild, as she reared up and kicked the stall door.

Iris hollered, "No! No!"

The barn was dim. There were a few overhead lights but Iris rarely turned them on. Light came in through cracks and she realized she'd left the barn door ajar. She looked at the entrance. In the light stood two big dogs. No, wolves! They growled deep in their throats and their ears stood straight up. Iris closed the door to Joshua's stall. Cookie couldn't get out and she didn't think the wolves could get in. Iris had never seen a wolf. Their teeth were showing and they sniffed the dirt floor moving close to the ground towards the stall door. Iris wouldn't be able to get out until they left. Where was her father when she needed him? She thought about guns. If Cookie or Joshua was threatened, could she shoot one of these wolves? The only thing she could use for a weapon in the stall was a pitchfork. What if Martha Rose or Merry decided to come out to the barn? What would she do then? How could she warn people?

Farmers had bells they rang when there was a fire or emergency. When you heard a bell clanging everyone looked for smoke and the men would take off to help. She couldn't get to the bell, could she? It hung high outside the barn door. If she could climb up into the loft she could lean out the hayloft door and hit the bell with a pitchfork.

She thought about this. Looking up, Iris saw that she could

climb up on the slats in Joshua's stall, walk around on top of the slats holding onto the beam above her until she came to the loft ladder, then climb up. She knew there was a pitchfork in the loft. Could wolves climb ladders? She had to warn her family. She climbed the slats and balanced on the top. She held onto the low stall beam and make her way to the ladder. She knew she could. As she began her perilous journey the wolves sank low to the ground and growled louder and lower. It was worse than her nightmare. She reached the ladder and climbed onto it. When she got to the loft she threw a hay bale down at the wolves. They slunk close to the ladder, sniffing. Cookie barked ferociously.

Iris grabbed the pitchfork, lay down, leaned out the loft opening, and whacked the bell. Once, twice, three times. Her mother came to the back door. Iris yelled, "Stay inside! There're wolves in the barn!" She hit the bell three more times.

By now, she heard the wolves snuffling at the ladder. One of them climbed on top of the hay bale she had thrown and was trying to climb the ladder. She thought, the only weapon I have is a pitchfork. She held the pitchfork with the handle end leading down the ladder. Maybe she could push them off. One wolf was close to the top of the ladder when she swung the end of it at the creature and it sailed off in a lump on the floor. It reared its head and roared. The second wolf started up the ladder, the first one, right behind. This time Iris pointed the sharp prongs down the ladder. When the wolf got close she jabbed and caught the animal in the throat. Both wolves fell to the floor, one of them bleeding and shrieking, the pitchfork imbedded in its throat. The uninjured wolf began to climb towards her. Iris heard a human cry, a woman's voice, "Aii-eee!" Laughing Sky stood in the doorway of the barn, bow and arrow cocked. When the startled wolf looked at her she let the arrow loose. Iris heard the thrum of the heavy gut string then the wolf's gurgle. A car door slammed and Earl and Oscar ran into the barn. Iris sat down on the hay and cried. In a second the barn was full of people, her mother, Martha Rose, Merry, her father, Oscar, and Earl, and Laughing Sky, staring up at her. The only person Iris remembered though, was Oscar, who climbed the loft ladder, sat next to her, held her, and let her cry.

Earl, Oscar, and Laughing Sky stayed for dinner. Afterwards, Earl and Horace dug two graves behind the barn. Martha Rose said, "We're gona' have a cemetery out there."

Later that evening, Laughing Sky took Iris into the kitchen, had her sit in a chair, and knelt in front of her. "Over a year ago I looked at you and called you, "The Bold One." You proved it in the cave last July and you proved it today. Iris, you can do anything."

"But why did you have your bow and arrow?" asked Iris.

"I was target practicing behind my cabin shooting pine cones off a log. I heard the bell and came running."

"You always know when I need you. How do you do that?"

Her friend wrinkled her forehead, lowered her head and murmured, "I just know."

Iris saw Oscar in the kitchen doorway. His arms were spread out from his sides, "I've never known anyone so brave," he said.

NOVEMBER

Laura Ellen looked out of the kitchen window into the gray morning light, her warm flannel robe smoothed across her stomach. Iris was up early seated at the kitchen table with her geography book open before her. The kitchen was clean and silent for a change. Her mother filled the coffee pot and measured out grounds. Then she relaxed in the rocker to wait for the coffee to perk. Iris looked at her mother. The smell of coffee didn't bother her anymore.

There was a light tap on the kitchen door. When Laura Ellen opened it, there stood Laughing Sky, eyes bright.

"Goodness gracious, is everything all right?" asked Laura Ellen, "What a bitter cold morning!"

Iris looked up from her book. Laughing Sky's face was bright from the cold, but her smile could melt lake ice.

"Sorry to break into your morning, but I could not wait." The words rushed out of Laughing Sky's mouth.

"It's never too early here," said Laura Ellen.

Laughing Sky took her coat and boots off at the back door, came into the kitchen put her arms around Laura Ellen, and hugged her. She hugged Iris too, and pulled a chair close. She leaned over, took one of Laura Ellen's hands in hers, and sat next to her friends at the table. "I saw your kitchen light and I knew in an instant you were the one I should tell." She took a deep breath and began, "I had a vision! A feeling of anticipation has been with me for a week or more, but early this morning I had a vision of a man walking down a dirt road singing! I feel like I'm sixteen! Imagine a grown woman of twenty-five dreaming like a girl, the sun shining, the man singing, and...I am there. The man walked from a long way off. Our eyes had paths of light that met."

Laura Ellen put her hand on Laughing Sky's shoulder, "What a way to wake up! Let me pour you a celebratory cup of coffee."

Iris narrowed her eyes, leaned forward, and added, "Maybe the man in your dream is on his way right now!"

Laughing Sky added, "He had a blonde beard and pack like an explorer," she explained. She leaned towards Iris and her mother. "I will be ridiculed if my dream is passed from mouth to mouth. Keep this a secret between us, please?"

Horace limped into the kitchen yawning. When he saw Laughing Sky he stopped mid-stretch and asked, "Everything all right?"

Laura Ellen answered, "Of course." She looked at her shaggy-haired husband. "Laughing Sky came to wish us good morning."

"Well, good morning," Horace said.

"Good morning to you," answered Laughing Sky. "I must go." She slipped into her coat and boots and vanished as quickly as she had appeared.

"Did I miss something?" asked Horace.

"Yes," answered Iris.

"Well, your friend's happiness is contagious. Look at the two of you sitting there grinning!"

Eight inches of powdery snow fell later that morning. After lunch Iris took a loaf of raisin bread to Laughing Sky's cabin. Laughing Sky's smile was constant. Try as she might, she couldn't erase it.

"When is One Deer coming home for the holidays?" Iris asked.

"My good brother comes today. I'll treat him to some of this beautiful bread from your mother. Please thank her for me."

Iris said, "Well, I have to go. Mother wants Merry and me to wash windows indoors for our company. Will you come later for sledding, if she lets us out?"

"One Deer won't come until dusk, so yes. I'll come along this afternoon," she replied.

Years later, the Andersen family heard the story of Laughing Sky's afternoon trip from her cabin to the farmhouse at every Thanksgiving gathering. It went like this:

I followed Iris' early footsteps along the path. The sun had come out and it was blazing on the snow. I could hardly see. When I reached the drive to the house, I heard singing. Still as a deer, I shaded my eyes. Walking down the drive was a man. At first all I heard were snatches of melody, then I saw blond curls and a beard. I jerked and flew back to my cabin fast as a sparrow! My scarf blew off behind me and I left it on the path. I giggled all the way to my front door.

Luke's version went like this:
I walked a mile from the train depot to the farm road. I hitched my bundle higher and started to sing: "Black is the color of my true love's hair"... I saw the farmhouse smoke streaming from the chimney. Then there was a woman running, a red scarf trailing behind her, then falling in the snow. I couldn't help smiling. I walked up to the house grinning like a kid, with that red scarf in my hand.

When Iris opened the kitchen door to let Cookie out, there was a bearded man with a knapsack on his back and red scarf in his hand standing on the stoop. The instant he saw her he held his finger to his lips. This had to be Uncle Luke! She held the door open for him, and he snuck in. Her mother was at the stove stirring corn pudding for breakfast. Martha Rose entered the kitchen, saw her uncle with his finger to his lips, and stuffed a braid in her mouth so she wouldn't laugh. She sat at her place at the table. Luke moved to the rocker, took off his back pack with care, and held it in his lap. Just then Laura Ellen tuned from the stove and saw him, "Luke!" she whooped. "You shouldn't startle a pregnant woman. Oh, I'm so glad to see you!" She took two long strides, hugged her brother-in-law's shoulders and gave him a peck on his cheek. "My, you are a bearded scholar!"

Luke answered, "Hey, there's a watermelon under your apron," he said. "Lord, you are gorgeous!"

Martha Rose asked, "What's 'gawgeous'?" she asked.

"Ah-ha, the young princess!" said Luke. "Come here, and

let me squish you to pieces."

"No. No. No. I don't like squishes," replied Martha Rose.

Horace hurried into the kitchen from the barn, flung off his gloves, and grabbed his brother in a bear hug. The two men thumped one another on the back, looked long at each other, and hugged again. "I saw your bags by the back door. I can't believe it, you're home."

Martha Rose came forward and tugged her father's pants leg. "Daddy, Daddy, there's something wiggling dat bag," Martha Rose whispered.

Luke's face changed from grin to sweet smile. He rolled his eyes and held the pack in front of him. "All right. Everyone sit down." He took the rocker again and put the pack lengthwise in his lap. It began to squeak.

"See?" said Martha. "Somethin's in dere."

Luke unlaced a leather thong, reached into the bundle, and pulled out a blanket-wrapped parcel. As he began to unwrap it more squeaking came from the package on his knees. The Andersens leaned near. A small black-haired baby yawned, put a tiny fist in its mouth, and began to make noises like Merry's lamb did when it sucked on its bottle. The baby's hair stuck out in every direction and her skin was the color of apple butter.

Luke looked at his dumbstruck family. "This is my Daughter, Anna, true daughter of Ariel and Joseph Many Stars." Luke handed the bundle to Horace. "Greet your niece, Brother," he said.

Horace took the infant in his arms. She opened two big black eyes and looked him fully in the face. "I think she just discovered a new continent," Horace said. Then he looked at his younger brother. "I suppose you do plan to tell us how you became father to an Indian baby. Not a tall tale, please."

Luke took Anna from his brother. "After I've changed her, I will tell all. Laura Ellen, may I change her on your bed?"

"Of course. And we have diapers." Then she reached up to take the baby from him. "Oh, let me, Luke. I need practice."

Luke said, "Well, I'm new at this and I need practice too, but be my guest."

The girls followed their mother into her bedroom, and crowded around the bed. Anna had on a flannel sack, and under that, two layers of flannel nightgowns. Her diaper was soaked. Once naked, the little girl lifted her feet, grabbed them and brought her toes to her mouth. Laura Ellen asked Iris, "Would you get a warm wash cloth, and Merry, would you get the powder from my dresser? Martha Rose, you sit right here and don't let her turn over." Laura Ellen sprang up and went to her dresser. "Here you are Anna Many Stars, your first dress." She had recently sorted baby clothes from Martha Rose's baby days. She held up a soft yellow night-gown and found two yellow knit booties. There were diapers in Luke's pack. She laid a clean one under the baby's bottom and let Merry sprinkle soothing powder on the baby's bare skin and rub it in.

"She's softer than anything," said Merry.

"She looks like cookie dough," said Martha Rose.

When the girls were done cooing and Anna's nightgown had been pulled over her head, Laura Ellen took a soft baby brush and smoothed her thick black hair behind her little ears. Then she hoisted the baby on her shoulder and they went into the kitchen.

Luke stood and took the baby from Laura Ellen. He nuzzled the baby's round nose with his beard and she took two fistfuls and pulled. "Hello, lovely Anna. You smell like a girl," he said.

He took a seat and put a bottle of warm milk into Anna's mouth. She sucked like a piglet, put one hand on the bottle, and one on Luke's hand and looked up at him.

"I think it's story time," said Horace.

Luke sighed and held Anna closer. "All right. Anna has been legally adopted by me. I wish this was an easy story," he said. He fell silent and watched the baby. He began, "Anna's mother and father were my neighbors and closest friends. Joseph was older and like a brother to me. We hunted together, fished, told stories about our families and how we grew up, and sat in comfortable silence. Ariel was like that, too. Quiet, full of calm. I saw Anna the morning she was born. The midwife had been with them all night. Joseph came leaping across the meadow that separated our cabins. I was the first person to know. I became her godparent." Luke eyes dimmed, but he continued, "Anna was with her parents the night they were killed in an automobile accident. I was at home grading papers. I looked up sharply and knew something was wrong in the world."

"Just like Martha Rose does," interrupted Iris.

Luke looked over at his youngest niece. "I bolted from my cabin to theirs. It was ten o'clock at night and their truck was gone. I knew this was a bad sign. Anna was two weeks old and they never were out at night. I got in my car and drove towards town, and saw their old truck in a ditch. They had hit a tree and been killed instantly. Ariel's door had opened and she'd fallen out. Two other cars stopped. I hollered, 'There's a baby here! There's a baby!' I moved Ariel to look at her face and under her, clamped in her arms was Anna who looked up and began to wail. Both Ariel and Joseph were dead. In their will, Ariel and Joseph named me as guardian and with consent and many meetings of the Bureau of Indian Affairs, I became a father. The staff there knows me well, and knew what good friends I was with Ariel and Joseph, and odd though it may seem to you, they deemed me worthy of fatherhood. I'm still in shock. There was no way I could call and say, 'Hey, I'm a daddy! I didn't know what to say in a letter. Plus, I've been busy." He looked at his brother. "I thought that if I called you'd try to talk me out of it."

Martha Rose broke a long silence, "When's her birfday?"

Luke smiled at the little girl, "August first," he said.

"So, she's three and a half months old," said Laura Ellen. "Look how she adores you, Luke."

All through Luke's story, Anna kept her eyes on his face.

Luke said, "Horace, I need a lift to the depot for my other suitcases. I think I can leave Anna well attended."

"Look, she's sleeping," said Martha Rose in a hushed voice. "Can she sleep with me?"

Horace picked up his youngest and hugged her. "One day I know you and Anna will be sleeping buddies but remember, we have a cradle polished and ready. You can sit with her and rock it."

"I will," promised Martha Rose.

Horace turned to his brother. "Luke," he said, "I admire what you did. I admire it enormously, but you do know how difficult it will be to raise a girl child alone?"

"Got any ideas, big Brother?" asked Luke.

"Get a wife," piped up Martha Rose.

"I'll tell you what, Niece. You find me one, and I will marry her!"

Laura Ellen added, "Oh, Luke, don't give Martha Rose ideas. We don't know how she does it but she makes things…well, happen. I get weak thinking about it."

That evening, Iris and her father dried dishes together. He remarked, "I hope your mother can take the bedlam that's about to occur tomorrow. She's tired as a rock."

He nodded towards the living room where Laura Ellen rocked sleeping Anna, almost asleep herself.

"Oh, Daddy, we'll all help, and Laughing Sky will be here with One Deer. I can take good care of everybody! Plus, a lot of the work's been done."

Three pies sat on the kitchen counter, an apple pie, pumpkin pie, and raisin pie.

The rolls waited to be heated in the morning, and the turkey was ready to go in the oven first thing. Tomorrow would be a big day at the Andersens. Iris remembered the pecan pancakes they had eaten for Thanksgiving the year before, their first Thanksgiving in Harmony.

The next morning Iris came into the kitchen. Her mother's cheeks were pink from the oven heat. "Mother, you're hot as the turkey! What can I do to help?"

"Oh, Iris, I've never had so much help. Your father put the turkey in the oven and Uncle Luke made the dressing early when Anna first woke. I'll lie down after lunch. You and Merry can set the table with your grandmother's china after breakfast.

Just then the kitchen door opened, and Horace and Luke came in from the barn, red-faced with frosty eye lashes. Luke's white beard made him look like an old man. As he defrosted and began to drip, Laura Ellen gave him a towel to dry off. "Oh," she said, "We'll be so lonesome when the holiday is over. I enjoy your company so much and the girls have a new 'toy' to entertain them. I must say, Luke, you have your hands full."

Horace spoke up, "You certainly do, brother. You must be highly regarded in Bemidji for this adoption to have gone smoothly. How's this going to change your writing and teaching schedule?"

"Oh, I'm not as much of a hermit as you imagine, Big Brother," Luke said. "I'll just take a couple of these nieces home with me to help out."

Iris asked, "Mother, where is Laughing Sky? She said she'd be here early. Do you want me to go over and get her?"

"No. One Deer got home late. They'll be here in plenty of time. Don't worry. Everything's on time. Dinner is at four o'clock."

Iris and Merry put all the leaves in the dining room table, laid the good lace cloth in place and, as Iris set the dinner plates around, Merry added place cards she had made and decorated. The girls made many trips to the china cabinet for glasses, cups, saucers, and bread dishes. Iris thought it was the most beautiful table she'd seen.

She looked out the dining room window and saw Laughing Sky and One Deer coming across the pasture, their hands full of boxes that held their contribution to the dinner. Iris ran to open the kitchen door. "Here they are," she announced. Again the kitchen was full of talk and laughter and more coats were added to the full hooks at the back door.

Horace looked around. "Where is Luke? Well, I do have a little brother named Luke, who will show up when the spirit moves him...just like old times."

"Horace, I think the turkey is ready to be carved," said Laura Ellen. "Let's start putting the food in bowls and carry them into the dining room."

"That sounds like a job for a logistical expert and I think that means me," said One Deer. "Iris, show me where the plates are and you and Merry can help."

"What about me?" asked Martha Rose.

"You ask everyone what they want to drink," suggested Iris. "Then we'll know if they need a cup and saucer or glass."

Luke came down the stairs with Anna in his arms as Martha Rose went into the kitchen to take orders. "What do you want, Uncle Luke, coffee or milk?" she asked. "And where have you been, anyway."

Luke yawned. "Anna wanted to play most of the night. Then she took a nap and so did I. What time is it? Did I miss something?"

Horace said, "You are amazing. The work is done and you show up like a genie out of a magic lantern. You did this when you were a boy. Come here, I want you to meet some friends."

Laughing Sky was at the stove stirring the turkey gravy. She turned to meet the newcomer.

"Hello," said Luke. "I saw you early yesterday morning," his voice faded away at Laughing Sky's gaze.

There was a brief silence in the kitchen and when the story was retold Horace claimed he saw sparks pass between the two young people.

Horace broke the silence, "Luke's our poet and teaches at Bimidji College. This is Laughing Sky, weaver, healer, neighbor, and her brother, One Deer."

Laughing Sky lowered her eyes and managed a quiet, "Hello."

Luke found his voice, "You're the woman who saved Merry's life. I've hoped to meet you and thank you and also for being here with the girls when my big brother fell. This family owes you a lot of gratitude."

Laughing Sky's face began to glow a dusky pink.

"My brother and his wife don't write much but every letter had you in it. You're a weaver? Anna's mother was a weaver."

Martha Rose closed in on Laughing Sky and circled her waist with her arm. "Anna's a baby. She's 'dopted, and Unca' Luke needs a wife."

Laughing Sky's eyebrows rose and she opened her mouth

in a soundless "Oh!" and turned to the stove. "I almost forgot the gravy!"

To her surprise the other people in the kitchen began to laugh.

One Deer took Luke's hand and didn't shake it but held it in his firm grasp looking into his eyes as he did. Iris noticed this. One Deer was as friendly as anything but like Oscar's father, he rarely looked directly into anyone's eyes.

Next there was a flurry as Oscar and Earl Runs Like Fox knocked on the kitchen door. Again the kitchen was a chaos of introductions and more coats, hats, and scarves hung on the rack by the door.

When the Andersens and their guests were seated, Iris could hardly believe the feast spread on their table: hot rolls, sweet potatoes, mashed potatoes, gravy, turkey with sausage dressing, corn pudding, wild rice, canned green beans from the garden, homemade applesauce, cranberry sauce, and pickled beets.

Horace said, "Let's join hands and thank God for our bounty."

Martha Rose placed one small hand in Laughing Sky's, and one in One Deer's. She beamed across the table at her Uncle Luke. "These are my best bestest friends," she whispered.

"Then we better add them to our list of thank yous, don't you think," her uncle said.

All hands joined, the family watched and waited for Horace to begin. He bowed his head, cleared his throat; cleared his throat again, then looked up at the expectant faces, his eyes shining, "I don't know where to start," he squeaked, and everyone laughed.

Laura Ellen beamed at him from the other end of the table and began, "Heavenly Father, you have blessed us with family and friends, and given us abundant pleasures in our life. Bless this food and all the dear hands that prepared it."

Iris watched Luke. His eyes never left Laughing Sky. She never lifted hers.

Martha Rose added, "Bless all the liddle children.'

Horace looked at his brother, "And please, don't forget poets who are responsible for connecting us to Your beauty, and give Martha Rose a hand in her latest quest. Amen."

"Amen," echoed around the table, along with laughs. Only Laughing Sky didn't laugh.

"I am going to find Unca' Luke a wife," said Martha Rose.

"Enough!" Luke roared. Everybody laughed, even Laughing Sky.

After the dishes had been cleared and the sour cream raisin, pumpkin, and apple pie leftovers had been stored, Luke rose, and said, "I hear Anna. She must want her own Thanksgiving dinner."

"Oh, no you don't," said Horace. "I will get that baby while you get started on the dishes! I've changed diapers longer than you have and I need to get in practice again. You're not escaping."

"All right," said Luke.

"You better roll up your sleeves, Uncle Luke," said Iris. "This could take a while."

In a few minutes, Horace appeared with Anna in his arms hungrily sucking her fist. "This may be the most pleasant baby I've ever met, since Martha Rose, of course." He took the baby and the bottle warmed by Laura Ellen. He barely got it in Anna's little round mouth before she began to suck noisily.

Laura Ellen took Laughing Sky by the arm, "Come meet Luke's new daughter." She pulled the pale yellow blanket from the baby's face. "This is Anna Many Stars Andersen."

Laughing Sky looked at the child, and her face warmed into a smile. "Aneen, little one." Anna looked at Laughing Sky and her eyes latched onto the young woman's face.

"Anna's parents died when she was two weeks old. They had chosen Luke to be her guardian," Laura Ellen explained in a quiet voice.

Laughing Sky leaned over her friend and whispered, "Do you remember my dream?"

"I've thought about it all day," said Laura Ellen.

"It happened like the dream only, only, it was Luke, this morning and I ran back to my cabin."

"No whispering among the ladies," said Horace.

"It's impolite," added Merry, looking on as Anna finished her bottle.

"She's done, Daddy," said Iris.

"I know but I'm not done holding her." He lifted the almost sleeping baby onto his shoulder, "How about a little burp, Anna?" He patted the tiny back with his big hand.

Luke called from the sink. "Whoo! We're done. I think this turkey pan should soak. Who's ready to work off desert?"

One Deer suggested, "Merry, Iris, Martha Rose, come help me hitch up our sled to War Bonnet, and we can ride down the drive in the snow."

"Yes, get the blankets too," said Merry.

"I'm in the front," shouted Martha Rose.

"You're always in the front," said Merry.

As dark fell, the yard light made a bright pool of snow by the barn. The children, weary from sledding and snowball battles, dragged their feet in their boots, and Luke announced, "Time to thaw. Let's go in." He picked up Martha Rose in one arm. "How about a bath to warm up?"

Merry and Iris trudged behind.

In the kitchen, Laura Ellen heated hot chocolate, and Laughing Sky sat in the rocker with Anna in her arms.

Luke took off his coat, pulled off his boots, then grabbed a chair to sit next to her. "Iris says you can throw a mean snowball. Why didn't you join us?" he asked.

Laughing Sky looked down at the baby without an answer.

"Will you come tomorrow?" he asked.

"I will," said Laughing Sky in a quiet voice.

Iris came up to them. "Daddy says tomorrow is broom ball on the pond eleven o'clock. Will you and One Deer come?" she asked.

One Deer spoke up, "You bet we will but watch out, my

delicate sister turns into a whirling demon on ice! She'll crack you on the shins in a minute," he added.

"Brother!" Laughing Sky seemed to wake up. "How could you say such a thing?'

Friday after Thanksgiving dawned clear and brittle. One Deer and his sister arrived early with their broom ball sticks. One Deer joined Luke in clearing the thick snow from the frozen pond. Laughing Sky took Iris and Merry on one more horse-drawn sled ride. Martha Rose stayed indoors with Anna. She declared "I am too cold to be out 'dere."

Before she left, Iris heard her father stumping about. "I think I'll go out and watch. Gotta' make sure they play fair."

"Oh, Horace," said his wife, "please take your cane and go slowly!"

"Yes, Mother," he answered.

Iris said, "I'll keep an eye on him," and hurried into the bitter wind.

When the children arrived, the broom ball field had been shoveled and swept. Team One consisted of Laughing Sky, Iris, and Oscar. Team Two was Merry, Luke, and One Deer. When Horace showed up he complained at not being able to play. Laughing Sky called, "Don't you worry, I'm mean enough for two!"

Iris had never seen this side of her friend. Laughing Sky was as at home on the ice as she was on solid ground.

Horace called, "I insist. I must at least be goalie!"

"No Daddy, you cannot fall down," hollered Iris.

"Now, you are my mother," he complained, then sat down on a log to watch the game.

True to her words Laughing Sky was fast on ice. The game was close until Luke drove in a point shoving Oscar into a snow bank.

Horace yelled from the side, "Foul! Foul!"

"Not in broom ball, Big Brother. Anything goes in broom ball, remember," Luke yelled back.

One Deer called, "Little Sister, you better make your move. We're closing in!"

Laughing Sky's rabbit fur had fallen off. She pushed the ball straight for the goal where Luke stood guard. Amazed at her move he moved to the left and she came straight at him as the ball went in, and she turned with a smirk for her brother. The wind caught her scarf and flung it against Luke's face. He pulled it away and smiled. "I love this game," he said. "I yield to my capturer, helpless."

A merry laugh sparkled from the young woman as she glided across the ice to congratulate her team.

After lunch of turkey noodle soup and rolls, the company settled by the fire drained of energy and cozy as puppies in a basket. Horace spoke up, "Luke, share a poem with us. What have you been writing this fall?"

Luke sat on the floor with Merry nestled near him. Anna cooed in Laughing Sky's arms moving her legs in a jerky dance.

"I've been working on a poem for a long time and couldn't make myself like it until this morning after Anna's first bottle. It's for Anna's mother, Ariel, titled, Weaver."

The weaver blends a strand of hair
into a blanket for her child.
Her bird-skeleton hands fly over the loom.

In dreams, a scarf leaves another loom
stretches miles
and wraps around me.

Filled with the presence
of another woman,
it warms me.

No one moved or made a sound. Even Anna was still. Laughing Sky kept her eyes on the child's face. The fire danced higher crackling in the quiet.

Laura Ellen spoke, "You've hypnotized us."

"Another one," said Iris.

"There is nothing a poet likes better than an attentive audience at his feet. You know, poems are meant to be read aloud, to be heard. I have one I wrote when I knew I'd be here for Thanksgiving. It's called, Three Little Girls.

Three little girls grow on a farm
like trees in a forest I know.
Supple as young pines, white as a birch,
they gain strength
from their roots as they grow.

When the wind blows, they dance for joy,
their arms pale in the moonlight.
Trees stand guard and protect
their home, while the girls
sleep through the night.

"Umm," said Laura Ellen, her hands still for a change, yarn and knitting needles resting in her lap.

Luke broke the quiet. "Who wants coffee or apple cider," he said getting up.

Iris followed him to the kitchen. "Uncle Luke, how long are you and Anna going to stay?"

Luke gave her a big hug. "I love your letters, Iris. Let's keep writing. Anna and I are returning to our cabin on Sunday. It's a long train ride this time of year."

"Can you stay longer?" asked his niece.

"Can't. I have a seminar to teach, and deadlines to meet. Do you think Anna and I could come back for Christmas?" he asked.

Iris yelled from the kitchen into the living room. "Uncle Luke's coming for Christmas!"

Her announcement was greeted with cheers.

Saturday at lunch Martha Rose complained, "Laughing Sky hasn't been here all day."

"One Deer is getting ready to go back to Cass Lake," said her Father.

"Why?" asked Martha Rose.

"He lives there," he said "He works on the reservation council."

"Then Laughing Sky will be all by herself," said the little girl.

"For a while," replied her father, with a twinkle in his eye.

Luke spoke up, "Since Anna and I are leaving early tomorrow, do you think I could go over and say goodbye this evening?"

Laura Ellen answered, "I definitely think you should go over and say goodbye."

"Iris, will you come with me?"

After dinner, Iris and Luke set out across the pasture with a lantern. Halfway to the cabin they saw a lantern approaching them. Laughing Sky and One Deer met them half way.

"We were coming to say goodbye to you and Anna," said One Deer.

"And we were coming to say goodbye to you," said Luke.

"Come home with us," offered One Deer.

Iris spoke up, "Laughing Sky has her own sleeping loft and you have to see her loom."

"I'm convinced," said Luke. "Lead the way."

The cabin had a large room that was kitchen and sitting room and held Laughing Sky's loom next to the window. A small bedroom and bathroom were off it. Sure enough, there was a log ladder leading up to a wide sleeping loft over the fireplace.

"That looks cozy," said Luke.

"It is," said Iris. "Sometimes Merry and I spend the night."

"Lucky girls," said Luke.

33

Laughing Sky stood by the window. There were two kitchen chairs and two wooden armchairs near the fireplace. A built-in cupboard held white dishes and glasses. They all sat down. Iris saw One Deer's pack near the door. "Are you ready to go?" she asked.

"I am," her friend answered.

Luke saw Laughing Sky's red scarf on a peg by the door. He walked over to it and let it run through his hands.

"Iris, why don't you and I poke up the fire? I damped it since I thought we were going to your house," said One Deer. "I think my sister and your Uncle have something to say to each other. This way we can pretend we aren't listening."

As Iris turned away, she saw her uncle take Laughing Sky's hand in his.

"May I write to you?" he asked.

Laughing Sky was silent, her head bowed.

Then she raised it and looked Luke straight in the eye. "What were you singing when I saw you walking down the drive early on that first morning?"

"It's a folk song, "Black is the Color of My True Love's Hair.' It's been in my head for a week," he answered.

She took a breath. "I dreamed, of a man with a beard, the sun at his back, singing to me the night before you came. Our paths are parallel."

"Until now," said Luke. "Now they've crossed."

Iris looked. They were holding hands.

"I do want to write to you," he repeated.

"I would reply," said Laughing Sky.

Early Sunday morning Luke and Laura Ellen stood in the kitchen. Anna was again in her basket, wrapped in blankets. Luke laid her on the table. "I'm looking for the rawhide teething ring One Deer gave me," he said, rummaging through his pack.

"Maybe it's underneath Anna."

He felt under the blankets that surrounded the baby and pulled out a long red scarf. "How did that get here?" he asked. "Did you put this here, Iris?"

"No," Iris said, shaking her head.

Laura Ellen put her hand on Luke's arm. "Laughing Sky was here early. It's her way of sending a little bit of herself with you two."

"This will get me through the long cold nights 'til Christmas," he said. "Tell her, will you."

Laura Ellen laughed. "Yes, I will. She'll love it."

DECEMBER

Martha Rose stood in front of Iris while her big sister brushed her short hair. "Don't forget the ribbon," she said, handing Iris several red strands. "Put them in with those pins so they won't fall out," she added.

Iris turned her sister to the mirror. "See how it looks," she said. The ribbons hung down on Martha Rose's shoulders.

"I like me. Dee-light-ful," the little girl said.

"Martha Rose, what made you cut off your braids? Can you explain it?" asked Iris.

"I wanted to see what I look like."

"And do you like it?" asked her sister.

"I do. When I'm growed up, I am going to have half short, half long hair, and nobody better laugh." The little girl looked out the kitchen window. "Snow," she announced.

Merry Columbine came in the kitchen covering a big yawn. She walked up to Iris, "Braid me, two braids," she said, handing Iris her brush.

"I feel like Mrs. Lucy's hair shop," said Iris. "I've been putting my ponytail up for three years all by myself."

"Ponytails are easy. Martha Rose, why do you have those ribbons hanging down?" asked Merry.

"I'm pretending they are hair."

"You look ridiculous," added Merry.

Martha Rose stamped one foot. "I look dee-light-ful!"

"What made you chop off your hair? It's a good thing Mother could cut it even. Your neck is going to get cold! Honestly, Martha Rose…"

Laura Ellen came into the room. "Girls, is that the best you can do? Can I hear a 'good morning dear sisters' from Merry and a 'thank you dear big sister' from Martha?"

Merry said, "Good morning, Martha Rose. You know, you could have real braids, long ones that hang over your shoulder like I do if you hadn't been silly."

Martha Rose turned her back on Merry. "Thank you, dear big sister," she said to Iris, and gave her a hug.

"You're welcome, dear little sister," said Iris.

Horace came in from outdoors. Steam rose from his wool coat. "Ah, my princesses all in one room!"

"Yes, Daddy, and I am beautiful," said Martha Rose, running to hug him.

"You certainly are," he agreed, flipping her red ribbons.

He hugged Iris next, and gave Merry a kiss on her cheek since she was holding still for her braids.

"I saw One Deer this morning," he said.

"Merry, hold still," said Iris.

"Just make one braid, then," said Merry.

"I know Laughing Sky is happy to have him home," said Laura Ellen.

"Now, when is Unca' Luke coming?" asked Martha Rose.

"Look at the calendar one more time," said her Father.

He and Martha went to the wall calendar by the back door. "Here's today," her father put a red diagonal line though the date with a crayon. "Here's the twenty-second with a red circle on it. Now, how many more days?" he asked.

Martha Rose put her finger on the twenty-second. "Two! Two days left and Unca' Luke and Anna will be here."

Her mother said, "I think you're more excited about Uncle Luke than you are about Christmas."

"I am. If I'm going to get him a wife he has to be here."

Later in the afternoon, One Deer knocked on the back door. Iris answered.

"Do you have a tree yet?" One Deer asked.

At the sound of his voice, all three girls left what they were doing and ran into the kitchen to greet their friend.

"No, not yet," answered Iris.

"Let's get one. Where's your Father?" he asked.

Merry said, "He's in the basement putting coal in the furnace. I'll get him."

In a minute, she and her father came up the stairs, Horace, still limping. "One Deer," he called out. "Merry tells me you're off to get a tree. Do you want me to come?" he asked.

"You and Laura Ellen stay here, and I'll take the girls out on the sled. There's a nice stand of firs near the river."

"Daddy, is that near the caves?" asked Iris.

"If it is I'm not goin'," said Martha Rose.

Horace answered, "No, not nearly that far." He leaned down to Martha Rose,

"Would you let me take you back to the cave this summer?" he asked.

"Not this summer. Not next summer," insisted the little girl.

One Deer spoke up, "You didn't get a chance to see them. I'll go with you, if you'll go. I know another entrance and it will be like a new place."

"Would you take us?" asked Merry.

"I'd go with you and your Father," said One Deer.

"I am not going into any cave anywhere, ever again, not with anyone," stated Iris flatly. She crossed her arms over her chest.

"I'll go if Iris goes," said Merry.

"Well, I'm not going."

"I might go with One Deer," said Martha Rose, putting her hand in his. "If he holds my hand the whole way."

"Girls," Horace began, "We don't need to decide today. Sorry the caves were brought up. Right now, who wants to go tree hunting?"

The five cold adventurers returned to the farmhouse with an enormous tree tied to the sled, a sack of pine cones, and branches to place on the mantel. As soon as the sled pulled around the house, the girls saw a black car next to the barn.

"Uncle Luke!" shouted Iris, jumping from her perch on the tree's trunk.

One Deer slid off War Bonnet's back and helped the other girls off the sled.

They rushed to open the kitchen door, shouting, "Anna, Uncle Luke!"

Her father called, "Stomp the snow off your boots, first,

then come in and take them off!"

Laura Ellen stood by the stove with Anna in her arms. The baby rested neatly on her protruding abdomen.

Iris called, "Anna, it's Iris, remember me?"

Martha Rose looked around. "Where's Unca' Luke?" she asked.

Her Mother answered, "He dropped Anna off, and immediately tore across the field to your cabin, One Deer."

"That was quick," said the young man with a smile. "You should see the pile of letters and poems on my sister's table. She's keeping the postman in business. Now, make way for the tree, it's a beauty."

He and Horace got the tree from the sled and carried it into the house.

"It almost doesn't fit," shrieked Martha Rose.

Laura Ellen laughed at her youngest child's excitement. "Now, it's Christmas," she declared.

Iris looked out the window. "Look! Here they come, Uncle Luke and Laughing Sky."

"Does the snow melt under their feet," asked her father.

Merry looked blankly at her father.

"One day you'll get it," said Iris.

"You are so uppity," replied Merry.

That evening, dinner was served near the tree. Laughing Sky held Anna while the baby slept, and Horace read from Charles Dickens,' A Christmas Carol. Uncle Luke knew all of 'Twas the Night Before Christmas and recited it with the help of the girls.

The fire in the fireplace crackled as One Deer added more wood.

Martha Rose requested, "Daddy, tell the naming story."

"Actually," he responded," we need to do some naming ourselves."

Iris chimed in, "Let's name our baby."

"I know his name," said Martha. "It's Benjamin. I told you and told you."

Merry said, "It might be a girl, you know."

"It ain't a girl," insisted her little sister.

"Isn't," corrected Merry.

Luke said, "I have an idea. How about a Biblical name, like Obadiah, or Hezikiah?"

"Oh, Uncle Luke," said Iris in exasperation.

"What about Susan," said Merry. "I wish I was named Susan. People spell my name wrong, and nobody would spell S-u-s-a-n wrong."

Iris said, "I suggest Susan Margaret, after our Grandma Margaret."

"How sweet," said Laughing Sky.

"What about Lucinda," said Horace.

"Daddy, are you bein' silly?" asked Martha Rose.

"Well, if it's a boy, like you insist, I think I'd like Benjamin Patrick. Benjamin Patrick Andersen is a distinguished name," said Laura Ellen. "The Patrick comes from your father's side of the family."

"It could be a girl," said Merry, "no matter what Martha Rose thinks."

Martha shook her head. "It's not a girl," she said slowly.

CHRISTMAS EVE

"Horace, Horace, where are you," Laura Ellen called into the barn.

"Here, Honey," replied her husband from Joshua's stall. "I'm giving Joshua and War Bonnet some Christmas oats and a good brushing."

"Luke has the girls occupied, so Iris and I are going over to Laughing Sky's before lunch. I promised her I'd visit. She's made something for Luke she wants us to see."

"Let me walk you over," said her husband, putting on his gloves.

"Horace, I will be fine. I'm not sick, I'm pregnant. Iris will look after me."

Her husband hugged her, "You do look rosy and cute. If you fall down, you'll roll."

"Thanks," said his wife.

"Have a good time, then. Be careful, for me," he added.

An hour later, Iris and her mother stood on Laughing Sky's porch saying goodbye. "We'll see you at 6:00 for dinner. Merry and Iris are excited to go to the midnight service with us." She looked at her daughter, "I'll make sure the girls lie down after lunch." She took one step down. "Luke will treasure the beautiful hanging you wove. It's a present worthy of a poet, perhaps your masterpiece, Laughing Sky." Without looking, she reached her foot for the final step, placed her boot squarely on a patch of ice and began to slip. "Oh!" she exclaimed, and reached for Laughing Sky's outstretched hand. Iris had walked a few steps towards the shoveled path. "Mother!" she called, and ran to the two women.

Both lost their balance and fell, Laura Ellen on top of Laughing Sky who had twisted her body to break her friend's fall.

They both lay still for a breath then Laura Ellen sat up. "Iris, where are you?" she asked.

"Here Mother. Give me your hand."

"Your father is going to be so mad at me. Ow, my wrist!" Iris' mother's left hand hung limp from her arm. She cradled it with her other hand, and Iris put her hands under her mother's arms, and pulled her up.

"Are you all right?" asked Iris.

"I think I am," answered her Mother. "Laughing Sky, how about you? Laughing Sky?"

Her friend lay on her side in the snow still as pain.

"Oh, dear," said Laura Ellen kneeling in the snow.

"I'll run for Daddy!"

"Hurry," said her mother.

Iris ran for home, hollering all the way, "Daddy! Uncle Luke!"

The two men met her at the back door, "Where's your mother?" asked her father.

"They fell! Mother's hurt her wrist, but Laughing Sky is on the ground..."

No sooner were the words out of her mouth than Luke bolted coatless across the snow.

"I need you here, Iris, with the children. Call Dr. Brenna and have him meet us at the hospital." Horace hurriedly put on his coat, gloves, hat, boots, and limped as fast as his mending leg would allow. "We'll call as soon as we can."

Later, Iris' mother told her all about the hospital visit. "Luke lifted Laughing Sky and carried her to the car. I stood on the cabin porch, holding onto your daddy with my good arm. I tried to move my wrist, and let out a yelp. Your father just had to say, "I knew something was going to happen. I knew it!

Her mother continued, "Then I apologized. I blurted out, oh, I'm sorry. We've ruined Christmas Eve. Try as I might not to cry, tears tumbled down my cheeks."

The three girls were there alone with Anna. Iris walked the baby until she fell asleep. Then she placed her on a blanket on the floor near the Christmas tree. When the telephone rang, she picked it up on the second ring. Martha Rose and Merry stood next to her.

"Iris, it's your dad," said her father. "Your mother has a broken wrist. Dr. Brenna is setting it. Laughing Sky has several cracked ribs and a broken collar bone. He wants her to stay overnight, but she's putting up such a fuss, that the doctor has agreed that if she comes home with us, we can doctor her here. We'll be home in an hour. Are you all right there?"

"Oh, Daddy! We're fine. Anna's asleep. Hurry up and bring them home. We'll be ready."

"Iris, you are a dream of a daughter. I'll bring the wounded home quick as I can."

"What'd he say?" asked Merry as Iris hung up the receiver.

"Mother has a broken wrist, and Laughing Sky has cracked ribs. They're coming soon!"

Martha Rose's eyes filled with tears. "Are they hurt bad?" she asked.

Iris knelt before her little sister and put her arms around her. "They'll get better. I promise. Let's get the sofa ready for Laughing Sky. Will you help?"

"Oh, yes," said Martha Rose. "She can have my pillow. I'll get it."

"Merry, go upstairs and get a sheet and blanket."

"I will. What else?" she asked.

"Let me think." Iris stood in the kitchen and looked around. "Let's move the table so they can carry Laughing Sky into the living room."

Both girls pulled the table a few feet closer to the sink.

"That's good." She turned on the outside light.

"Where's One Deer?" asked Merry.

"Hunting," said Iris. "Oh, no, how will we get word to him if Laughing Sky doesn't have a telephone."

"I can take a note and put it on his door that says, 'Come to our house right away.'" suggested Merry.

Iris said, "Are you going over there now? It's about to get dark."

"Then I better hurry," Merry said. "Remember the cave? I had to get help then. You told me I could do it, and I did."

At dusk, snow began to fall in large lazy flakes. The sofa was made up and Merry sat in the living room with Anna asleep in her lap while Iris and Martha Rose laid wood on the hearth for a fire.

"Laughing Sky will need to stay warm, won't she," said Martha Rose.

"Yes," answered Iris, "and you know how she loves the fireplace."

"It's getting so snowy I can't see the road," complained Martha Rose. "Are you sure, sure, sure they won't stay at the hospital?"

"Santa will give them a lift if they take much longer," said Merry. "We won't be able to go to church!"

"I guess not," said Iris. "I'm not counting on it, are you?"

Merry Columbine, answered, "I never stayed up 'till midnight yet."

"I know," said Iris, "Let's have our own Christmas Eve. I can read the Bible story, and Uncle Luke can play the guitar, and Merry, you can do the decorations, and…"

"And I can be the company," shouted Martha Rose.

"You mean, the congregation," corrected Iris.

"Oh, can I do that, too?" asked her little sister.

Just then, the back door opened, and Laura Ellen came into the kitchen, holding the door wide for Luke as he carried Laughing Sky into the room. One Deer came in behind them.

"One Deer, how did you get here?" asked Martha Rose.

"I got Merry's note, and went straight to the hospital," he answered.

Laughing Sky spoke up, "Let me stand up. I'm not crippled!"

The three little girls watched as their friend walked slowly, her left arm close to her side, and Luke, like a shadow next to her, holding her other arm. He and One Deer helped her settle on the sofa.

"Where's her arm," whispered Martha Rose.

Her father answered, "The doctor taped her ribs, and her arm is in a sling under her dress. She needs to keep still as possible. She broke her collar bone."

Martha Rose looked up at Iris who pointed to the horizontal bone on the top of her shoulder. "Oh, that must hurt so bad," she said. Her eyes filled with tears.

"It does," said Laughing Sky as she tried to get comfortable.

Laura Ellen sat in the rocker next to the sofa. "She really needs a warm nightgown. I can help her later, or maybe Iris can, to get her comfortable."

"Please don't make me get up again," said Laughing Sky sleepily.

Luke laid an afghan over her legs, and One Deer put a pillow next to her side to support her arm. The next thing Iris knew, her injured friend had closed her beautiful dark eyes and was asleep.

Her father said, "Let's go in the kitchen. The doctor gave her medicine to help her sleep, and it seems to be working."

Luke picked Anna up from her pallet on the floor, and said, "I'm going to change Anna, and put her down for the night. I don't think she missed me at all, thanks to you girls."

One Deer sat on the floor next to the sofa, and said, "I'll going to keep watch, if you don't mind."

"Please, make yourself comfortable, One Deer. We'll bring you something to eat and you can watch your sister sleep," said Horace. Then he turned to Iris and Merry. "Well, girls, your mother is in pain, too. We need to eat something, so will you give me a hand in the kitchen?"

Laura Ellen rose from the rocker and walked unsteadily into the kitchen. Iris rushed to her side, "Mother!" she cried, and hugged her gently as tears began to pour down her cheeks. "All I could think about was Daddy in the cave, and I didn't know what to do, again."

"You did exactly the right thing, again," her Mother said. "Exactly!"

Horace went to the back door and opened it. Snow swirled in gusts of cold wind. "We wouldn't have made it to the church tonight, anyway," he said, pushing the door closed.

Martha Rose pulled her mother's chair away from the table, and Laura Ellen sat down. "I can be your nurse," she said. "What can I get you? Do you need a pill?"

Horace knelt down in front of his youngest girl and hugged her.

"Remember when you fell and sprained your ankle in the cave?"

"I sure do. And it hurt! And I was cripple for a year."

Her father smiled, "Well, that's exaggerating it a bit, but remember how you wanted to be left alone for a while?"

"Yes, but Iris would not go away! And she kep' me company, and I'm gona' keep Mommy company and she won't get scared."

Laura Ellen pulled her little girl close with her good arm. "I love you, Pumpkin. Yes, you can be my nurse, and yes, you can get me something, a small pillow from my bed. I can rest my arm on it."

Martha Rose marched off to fetch the pillow.

After a simple meal of hot tea, cheese toast and apple sauce, Iris and Merry disappeared into the living room to make quiet preparation for their Christmas Eve service.

Laughing Sky slept, but Luke, Horace, Laura Ellen, Martha Rose Merry, and Iris were ready for the big event. Martha Rose put a white dish towel on the coffee table, Merry put the red Christmas candles on the table, and Iris lit them. Pine cones and holly were the decorations. Laura Ellen had put on her nightgown and warm robe, and had a cup of hot cider in her good hand. She rested her bandaged wrist on the pillow in her lap.

"First, we sing," said Iris. "Luke, start playing 'Joy to the World'."

Luke strummed a few chords, and they sang, "Joy to the World, the Lord is come, let earth receive her King..."

"Now, I will read the story of Jesus from our Bible," said Iris and began, "In those days a decree went out from Caesar Augustus that all the world should be enrolled...." she read the familiar passage from the book of Luke, and ended, "And the shepherds went with haste, and found Mary, and Joseph and the babe lying in a manger. And when they saw it they made known the saying which had been told them concerning this child: and all who heard it wondered at what the shepherds told them. But Mary kept all these things, pondering them in her heart." Iris closed the big Family Bible and hugged it to her chest.

"That was all I needed," said her mother, wiping her eyes with a handkerchief.

"What now, Daddy?" asked Iris.

"Well, since you're the preacher how about a prayer," he suggested.

"All right. Who wants to pray?" she asked.

"Me! Me! I want to," waved Martha Rose.

"All right," said Iris.

Martha Rose folded her hands under her chin. "Thank you for the world so sweet. Thank you for the friends we meet. Thank you for the birds that sing, Thank you, God for everything. Amen. Daddy, was that good?" she asked.

"A fine job, little one," her father said, holding her close.

"I would like to speak an Ojibway prayer," added One Deer.

"Good," said Iris.

One Deer held his hands slightly raised, palms up. "Grandfather, Great Spirit, heal our broken sisters. I pray for my friends gathered to celebrate the birth of your son who came into this world a naked infant, and became a man of peace. Teach us to be still, listen to your earth, and learn from your children. Keep the stars shining above the snow so that we might know our way in the darkness. Bless Mother Andersen and the child she carries, and reward her goodness. Let love grow like a tree with deep roots for Luke and my sister, and keep us all in your peace. Amen."

"You pray good," said Merry admiringly.

One Deer smiled, "I was inspired," he said.

Laughing Sky's eyes opened. "I heard every word."

47

Her voice was husky and soft. She held out a hand to Luke who moved to the sofa and held it with both hands.

"Another Christmas Carol," said Iris. "Quick, Mother's going to cry."

Luke left Laughing Sky and took up his guitar. "How about, O Little Town of Bethlehem," he said.

In the wee hours of Christmas morning, when the black sky became purple around the edges, Merry came into Iris' bedroom and poked her. "Iris, get up. Listen. Someone's awake downstairs." The two girls held their breath. "Let's go look."

Iris whispered, "Don't step on any cracks on the stairs."

"I won't," responded her sister.

The two shivering girls crept down the stairs. They looked into the living room. One Deer was covered by a blanket and lay on his back asleep by the fireplace.

Luke was on his knees next to the sofa where Laughing Sky lay with her eyes closed. Her hand was on his curly head, stroking him as if he were a pet. Luke was whispering and his words sounded like leaves. "I know this is not a good time, but my heart is so full it has to spill."

Laughing Sky lay silent. The two girls, still as statues, stared at the scene lit by orange coals in the hearth.

Luke continued, "I dreamed of you, Laughing Sky, your red scarf and black hair. I knew you before I met you, and loved you the minute I met your eyes at Thanksgiving. I want you to be my wife. My friend's deaths taught me that life is a precious gift. I want you to join me and Anna and begin our life together.

Merry grinned at Iris who put her finger to her lips.

Luke leaned his head nearer Laughing Sky.

"When the peonies bloom," she said, "I will be your wife when the peonies bloom." She smiled at him.

"You will? You really will?" Luke stood up and the girls moved against the doorway, out of sight. Luke put his hands in his hair and pulled it straight up.

"You really will?" He gave a little jump. Then he was on

his knees again, looking at Laughing Sky who had closed her eyes.

"When the peonies bloom," she whispered.

The two girls silently climbed the steps. They went into Martha Rose's room and woke her. "Martha Rose, we have a secret. Martha Rosie Posie, wake up."

Their little sister rubbed her eyes, then her nose, and looked at them.

"Luke asked Laughing Sky to marry him!" said Merry

"I know it," yawned the little girl. "I'm gona' carry the ring. It's all decided." She turned over and went back to sleep.

CHRISTMAS DAY

Laura Ellen smelled coffee. She looked out the bedroom window and saw snow falling in a thick blur. "Horace?" she called.

Her husband stepped into their bedroom as if he'd been standing right outside the door. "Are you all right?"

As she tried to sit up, Horace placed two pillows behind her back.

She held up her bandaged hand. "It hurts," she winced. "Merry Christmas anyway, husband."

"And Merry Christmas to you, wife," Horace said, kissing her forehead.

"Where are the girls? This isn't like any Christmas morning in memory."

"They were exhausted last night when I tucked them in. I thought I'd let them sleep. I imagine we'll hear them soon enough," said Horace.

"What about Laughing Sky? Is she still asleep? I should check on her." Laura Ellen sat up and put her feet over the edge of the bed. "This wrist is going to be a real nuisance," she said.

"Laura Ellen, you check on Laughing Sky and have a seat in the rocker. Let the men do Christmas this year," begged her husband.

Laura Ellen smiled and shrugged her good arm into her robe, slipped on her slippers, then walked to the kitchen. One Deer was seated at the table with a mug of coffee in front of him. He got up and went to the stove. "Good morning, Mother Anderson. May I pour a cup of coffee for you this Christmas Day?"

"One Deer, you must have been up all night! How's your sister?" asked Laura Ellen.

"Sleeping," he answered. "I have been sleeping also." He raised the coffee pot and looked at his friend.

"Yes, please. Coffee is what I need. It smells wonderful."

She noticed Anna sleeping in a bed of towels in the laundry basket beside One Deer's chair.

"I heard Anna making wake up noises, so I went upstairs and got her before she woke anyone else. I fed her a bottle and changed her diaper myself. That's a first for this bachelor!" One Deer laughed.

"I'm sure Anna didn't care. She is such a good baby. I hope she is always this peaceful. Where's Luke?" she asked.

"Asleep in the chair next to Laughing Sky."

Horace sat down and poured coffee for himself. "What a treat this is. I didn't think it was possible to have a quiet cup of coffee on Christmas morning…Oh, oh, I hear whispering on the stairs." He leaned back in his chair and directed his voice to the stairs, "Come on down, girls, we're breaking tradition this morning. Let's have breakfast before we open our gifts."

Three blonde heads appeared around the door. "May we look at Laughing Sky first?" asked Martha Rose?

Her mother answered, "Yes, quietly. Then come back."

All three girls tip-toed into the living room, stood silently by the sofa, and tip-toed back.

"Pull up your chairs," said their father. "This morning I'm serving pancakes with pecans from Virginia."

"Yummy, yummy," said Martha Rose, rubbing her stomach. "I'm hungry!"

Her father bent down and kissed her on the cheek, "Not only are you hungry, you are pink as the inside of a sea shell."

"Mommy says I'm dee-light-ful!" Quipped the little girl.

Merry Columbine said, "I hear something from the living room. Maybe Laughing Sky wants to get up. I can still hear Uncle Luke snoring. May I go look?"

Horace said, "One Deer, why don't you check on your sister and I'll take over pancake duty."

"I'll come, too," said Laura Ellen.

"No, Mother, let me help. I have two good hands," said Iris.

Under the tree were two doll-sized wooden beds with chintz bedspreads and flannel sheets. The tag on each, "From Santa." Merry Columbine looked puzzled.

Martha Rose said, "I'm gona' get my doll," and ran from

the room. Merry came to her mother and stood quietly, with one hand on her mother's knee.

"What is it, Merry Columbine?" her mother asked.

"Mommy, did Santa make our doll bed?" She asked.

"Why, well..." Laura Ellen dodged and hedged her answer. Merry interrupted her, "'Cause, I saw that flower material in your sewing chest. Mother, it's more beautiful because I know you made it. Don't tell Martha Rose. She's so young, you know."

Laura Ellen hugged her. "Merry Christmas, Sweetheart. I love you."

"I love you, too, Mommy, and Benjamin," she added, patting her mother's rounded front. "He's growing in there, isn't he?"

Laura Ellen looked over at Laughing Sky on the sofa. "You look more comfortable this morning," she said.

"I am, as long as I'm still," said Laughing Sky.

Luke brought a small box to her. "This is for you," he said. "Martha Rose, would you unwrap this for Laughing Sky?"

"I will!" Martha tore the red paper and green ribbon off in one stroke. "Easy!"

Laughing Sky opened the top of the box and held up a silver band with engravings on it. Luke said, "An Ojibway friend of mine is a silversmith. He made this for you. The symbols of running water were my idea. They could be ribbons, or a red scarf blowing in the wind. The rosemary etching is for "memory." I don't want you to forget me."

"Put it on my wrist, please," said Laughing Sky as she held up her good arm. The girls admired the shining silver circle. "When the peonies bloom," she whispered to Luke.

Laughing Sky smiled at Laura Ellen. "Look, Mother Andersen, my engagement present."

"Engagement! Luke, you didn't waste a minute!"

"Time's precious, and you know me, I'm impatient."

Horace spoke up, "When? I suppose you've set a date?"

"When the peonies bloom," chimed Merry and Iris, and laughed together.

"Hey! What's so funny," said Luke. "We're being romantic here."

Laughing Sky turned to Horace. "You know the sledding hill where the peony beds are? I want to be married there in June, if I may. One Deer will stand with me, and I will have these three lovely girls carrying peonies."

"What a Christmas!" said Horace. "Wait! There's a present here for my wife somewhere. He pulled a piece of string out from the mess of wrapping paper and handed it to his wife. "Follow this string, and it will lead you to your present."

"Oh, Horace, what now?"

"Just follow the string," encouraged her husband.

Laura Ellen took up the end of string and pulled it through her hand as she walked, following it.

Martha Rose advised, "Go in the dining-room, Mother!"

Laura Ellen did, walking around the table into the kitchen, and to the pantry door where the white line disappeared under the closed door.

"Hurry up! Open the door," called Martha Rose.

Laura Ellen saw a large framed painting on the floor. Horace picked it up for her and held the green and cream water-color up for inspection.

"Magnolias!" exclaimed Laura Ellen. "Did Erwin paint these?" she asked.

"She did," answered Horace. "I don't want Virginia to be too far away, ever."

Martha Rose said, "Mommy's gona' cry again."

Luke spoke up, "I have something for you, too. It's not from Virginia." He handed her a flat gift. "You can share this with Benjamin."

"It's a book! I can tell it's a book!" shouted Martha Rose at her mother's side.

Laura Ellen unwrapped the present and in her hands was Beatrix Potter's book, Benjamin Bunny. Oh, Luke. I love these illustrations! I sure hope this baby is a boy!"

"Big brother, here's something for you."

"Another book?" asked Horace.

"Not just 'another book,'" answered Luke.

Horace tossed the paper aside and held a book bound in deep blue cloth with leather binding. Printed in gold on the spine was the title, A Child in Harmony, by Luke Andersen.

"Luke. Your book." He grabbed his brother and hugged him hard. "You said it would come out in spring."

"The publisher wanted it out by Christmas. I can't tell you how busy I've been."

"I'm going to sit here and read it right now!" said Horace.

"Daddy! Not now!" wailed Martha Rose.

"Look," Horace said. He held up the book to the dedication page and read:

"For those who keep Harmony, Horace, Laura Ellen, Iris, Merry Columbine, and Martha Rose."

"Luke, I'm touched," said Laura Ellen, wiping her eyes.

"Here's a present from Laughing Sky," called Merry. "It's for you, Uncle Luke."

"For me?"

"Yes, silly!" said Merry. "When you come at Christmas, you get presents!"

As Luke untied the gift, Laura Ellen smiled at Laughing Sky.

It was a woven wall-hanging with red ribbons and blue wavy lines woven together. Laughing Sky said, "The gray rising thread is the fire that will rise from our home. The three stars are you, Anna, and me. There are strands of my hair, yours, and Anna's woven into the stars."

Luke carefully hugged his future wife. "I have never had such a gift as you!" he said.

Horace finally said, "If we are going to have Christmas dinner, Luke and One Deer, we better get started. Laura Ellen, you sit right there looking beautiful and give us instructions."

The snow continued to blow. It peered in the living room windows and leaped gaily in the wind. It built layers of magic crystals on the window sills, and drifted onto the path to the barn. From the road, the house glowed like a Christmas card, smoke rising from the chimney into the dark sky.

Can you hear the carols? Horace has tuned his guitar and they're singing, "Silent night, Holy night, all is calm, all is bright."

JANUARY

A new year: 1939. Grandpa died last year. I will never forget that January. Will somebody die this year? I know somebody is going to be born this year, and Uncle Luke, Laughing Sky, and Anna are getting married in June! They are going to build a house on the road behind our barn. Who will live in her cabin? Luke and Anna have gone home. Laughing Sky is back in her cabin with One Deer waiting on her. I love to visit. I know Laughing Sky misses her loom. I see her glance at it. It will be a long time before she can weave again, or lift anything.

I'm not worried about Mother, not her wrist, anyway. She made bread for New Year's Eve dinner last night. Daddy only had to help her punch it down and knead it. She is getting big! I can put my hands on her big belly and feel hard kicks. She wasn't this big with Martha Rose, I know that. Maybe little sister is right. Maybe it's a boy!

Iris closed her journal, a gift from Uncle Luke. He said that every good writer needs a journal for seeds for future writing. She'd written in it every day. She'd also written letters to Uncle Luke and Anna, Grandmother, and Dorothy. You have to write a letter to get a letter, that's what Mother says. It was no problem for Iris. She loved to write.

School would start on January 5th. There were four days left in her Christmas holiday. Today she would go to Julie's house and spend the night. It would be her first night away from the farm, and her first night at Julie's house. She'd only slept in four houses: her old one on Brook Road, Grannie's, and Dorothy's, and now her farm house. She wondered what a night at Julie's would be like. Julie lived in town. Her father owned the creamery. Her parents were older than Iris' mother and father, and she didn't have any brothers or sisters. Iris couldn't imagine being an only child.

Julie's father was bald, short and round. He and Julie came to pick Iris up in his truck. When Julie's dad shifted gears, there was a grinding noise Iris had never heard in a car before.

"Big storm comin'," said Julie's dad. "Big one."

At three o'clock in the afternoon the sky was dark. Winter days were short. Even in her second winter in Harmony, early dusk still surprised Iris.

"When we get home we're staying put," he added.

"We're going to draw and play Old Maids," said Julie. "We'll have a fire in the fireplace, and Iris, you can lead Charades, and Daddy will tell a story. It's going to be fun. We get to sleep upstairs."

Iris had visited Julie's house many times. It was next door to the post office on Main Street. There were big trees out front and a garden in the back. Julie's Mother spent a lot of time in the garden. Her dark hair was streaked with gray. She looked more like a grandmother than a mother. She quilted, and was the leader of a library group for grown-ups who like to read. The house had a big front porch and an outer door and an inner door, like most Minnesota houses. You took your coat and shoes off before you entered the house. Sometimes Iris forgot.

Soon as they walked in Iris smelled lemon bars baking.

Julie said, "Yum, lemon bars! Iris, let's take your bag upstairs where we'll sleep. Have you been up there?"

Julie couldn't stop talking.

When they'd climbed the narrow stairs, there was a big open room. It had a sloped ceiling because of the roof. In fact, it sloped on the front and back of the house, so it looked like they were sleeping in a tent. A large puffy bed stood at the tallest part of the room, and there were bedside traveling trunks with a lamp on each, but that was all that was in the room. It was chilly up here.

Julie said, "We'll use three quilts tonight. It feels good to have all those heavy covers on. I love to sleep in the cold, don't you?"

"I guess," said Iris, turning around. "What's out here?" She looked out the East window and there was the Post Office. Mr. Halker ran it and only had to walk next door to get to work. Oscar and his Father lived two houses away. Oscar and Earl "keep to themselves," as Julie's mother often said. She had been good friends with Oscar's mother. Iris hoped she would talk about her. She walked across the room, and looked out of the West window. In the blackening sky she saw dark clouds. It was a wind-dizzy day. Trees writhed and snow spiraled and swirled.

"Your Dad was right about a storm. Look."

Julie came to the window, and she and Iris watched lightening twitch in the distance. "We don't have lightning in January," she said.

"You do now," answered Iris.

Julie's father was listening to the radio. His wife, Elsie, stood near him, drying a wooden spoon with a dish towel. When the girls came in he clicked the radio off.

"What did the weather say, Daddy?" asked Julie.

"Oh, not much," he said, but Iris knew he was hiding the truth. Julie's mother turned a bright smile on the girls and said, "Maybe we could move some cushions to the cellar. I don't think we're in danger but it might be a good idea, just in case."

"Just in case?" repeated Julie.

"Yes."

A blazing bolt of lightning lit the snow covered yard. Thunder cracked immediately, a sharp breaking sound. The lights went out. Julie's mother let out a yelp.

"Julie, grab a candle and head downstairs," her father shouted over the echo of thunder.

"Iris, take my hand," Julie called. She picked up a candle from the table, struck a match on the side of the box, and the dark was lit by a brave little light.

The four of them descended the cellar stairs.

"Daddy, how can it thunder in January? Thunder storms are for summer!"

"When we were kids we called it Thunder Snow. It sounds worse than it is. It's a tornado with snow."

Iris listened. The wind was a constant blur of noise. It moaned, whistled, and blustered around the house. The eye-level basement windows were blocked by snow. Without lights, it reminded Iris of her first tornado when she was hunkered in the school basement with her classmates.

"Wallace, I don't like it," said Julie's mother. "There are more candles stored in the cupboard near the coal box. I'll get a few." She carried a candle and walked towards the furnace room.

Wallace raised his head. "What's that?"

Iris and Julie got still. There was a rattling sound then thunks on the front door.

Julie's dad asked, "Now what? There's someone banging on the door! Who in the world is out tonight?" Julie's father hurried up the stairs.

He came down the stairs with Oscar. The boy had on his deer skin mittens and his face was scarlet from the wind. Oscar looked around the cellar, saw Iris and Julie sitting on their quilts and asked, "Iris, what are you doing here?"

"Spending the night," she answered.

"You sure picked a good one!" replied Oscar. He turned to Mr. Gonner, "My father sent me to make sure everything's all right over here."

Julie's mother walked in and answered for her husband, "Yes, we're fine. Oscar, what about you two? I can't believe your father sent you out in this storm to ask about us! Do you need candles?" She held out a box of them.

"Thanks. We've got kerosene lanterns. Dad says the storm is going to get worse. You know…he can't stop being grateful for last February. All that soup and bread you brought over, and the wood you chopped, Mr. Gonner."

"Oscar, go home and be safe. We're fine. You and your Dad could join us. What about that?"

"Oh, no, Dad would never do that. You know him."

"Yes, we do," sighed Mrs. Gonner. "Well, go on, we'll be thinking about you. Thank your Father for his offer of help."

Mr. Gonner followed Oscar up the stairs. Iris heard the front door close.

"I feel like a tramp down here sleeping in the cellar," said Julie.

"A tramp should be so lucky. Remember the lemon bars," said Julie's father as he came into the room.

"Look at our nest," Julie said.

She and Iris had spread a canvas cloth on the floor, and covered it with cushions, a quilt, and had placed two quilts on top. There was a wooden box with a candle on it next to the made-up bed. A deck of cards sat next to the candle.

"All the things we planned to do, cards, charades, stories, we can do here," Julie announced. "We've got all the light we need."

Iris could see Mrs. Gonner's washing machine at the other end of the cellar. It was like her mother's, round with wringers at the top. Mrs. Gonner had a clothes line in her cellar like Iris' mother.

Mr. and Mrs. Gonner went up the stairs. They returned with trays of chicken and dumpling soup, rye bread, and a plate of lemon bars. "In all my years, this is the first time I've had a cellar picnic," said Julie's mother.

"Daddy, tell us a story while we eat," said Julie. "Tell the bull and the harmonica one."

"Julie, you've heard that yarn since you were three years old."

"Iris hasn't."

"I'd like to hear it if you want to tell it," said Iris.

"I'll see if I can spin it one more time," said Mr. Gonner.

"It's true, all of it," said Julie.

"One story-teller at a time, please," added Mrs. Gonner.

Mr. Gonner put his soup bowl down on a tray, rubbed his calloused hands together and began, "When I was a boy I loved to fish. I'd rather fish than eat. My two uncles raised me on a farm not far from here, Uncle Howard and Uncle Hayes. My mother died when I was three, and my father had died in the war. My uncles let me do most anything I wanted. Some of it was good, some not good for a twelve-year-old boy. I could roamed everywhere. I quit school when I was thirteen, never wore shoes in the summer, made my own fishing poles and lures, and took off when the spirit moved me. One August, I was eager to get down to the river. There was a long way and a short way. The long way took me 'round Mr. Gudykundst's place. The short way took me through his pasture. He had cows and a bull. The cows were no problem. The bull was. I've known bulls, had some myself, but this bull, well, I guess you'd say he was territorial. In summer the cows gathered at one spot in the field. In the center was an oak tree. It was a great climbing tree. It stood in the halfway point between the barbed wire fences. The cows loved that shade. The bull loved that dark cool place too. I always said to myself, Wallace Gonner, run to that tree, scare off that bull, wait a bit, then shimmy down and haul yourself off to the other side of the pasture, slip under that fence, and you're on your way to the big ones at the river. Now, I played harmonica since I was five years old. I had been down at the pasture fence in the past, and played harmonica for the cows. I always had it on me. That bull, he'd snort and paw the ground, head down, and come lunging at the fence. He didn't like my music. Well, I thought that if I could get to the tree, get up in it, and play, he'd run off mad. On this particular day I was thinking of swimming and fishing, so I decided to head for the tree. I got my harmonica out, made some awful loud wheezy sounds, and sure enough, the cows shuffled off, and the bull, too. The bull didn't go far. He glared at me. I lay down in the grass and wiggled under the fence, fishing pole and tackle box with me, harmonica in my pants pocket. All of a sudden, the tree looked far off. I'd decided what I was going to do though, so I took off at top speed. I dropped my fishing rod and tackle box at the foot of it. I couldn't climb and carry them. I got up to a branch about ten feet off the ground when that bull charged. I hung on for my life. The tree shook and shivered but I held tight. The bull walked off, shaking his head, so I took out my harmonica and wheezed some more. That bull was about twenty feet away, swaying and stomping the ground. He took another run at the tree and tore up my fishing rod with his hooves, and smashed my tackle box with his head. I wondered if my uncles would hear the commotion or at least my harmonica. They were most likely off in the field. They rarely checked on me. I was on my own, little Wallace, up in a tree with a bull stompin' around some kind of fierce. At times, the bull would look up at me, and wander off, then charge back, daring me to jump down and head for the fence. I began to think he was smarter than I was. Each time he wandered just a little farther off than the last time. I thought to myself, wait. Be patient. Give him time. I thought I was a good judge of distance. When he was far enough away, over halfway to the end of the pasture, I jumped down and ran like the dickens! I could hear his hooves and snorts behind me. I reached the fence, rolled under it with a r—i—p from my shirt. I stood up, red-faced, sweaty, and there he was, on the other side of the fence, pawing, mad as a hornet. I shook all over. I remembered the river. Yes sir, water! I took one long look at my mangled fishing rod and tackle box. I could make another rod and more lures. Uncle Hayes would help me. I headed for that water hole, shed my pants and ruined shirt, and walked in until I was up to my neck. I decided then and there, I'd take the long way home."

Iris clapped. "That really happened? You really did play a harmonica and scare a bull? How did you dare go under the fence?"

Julie spoke up, "I asked him the same thing. Daddy acts like it was nothing."

"Well, it's just the way things were then. My uncles turned me loose, and I learned a lot. When I remember the danger I was in, I shudder. That's why your Mother and I won't let you out of our sight. No ma'am. No bulls for our Julie."

He smiled at his daughter. Iris thought it was the best smile ever.

After the story and lemon bars, they played Old Maid. Mr. Gonner won. They played again, and Julie won. Iris said, "Don't you think company should win?"

They all laughed. Mrs Gonner said, "Julie and her Dad take games seriously."

Julie's Mom and Dad took the dishes up and left them in

the sink. "I'm not doing dishes in the dark," said her mother.

The wind continued its furious dance.

Julie and Iris pulled quilts over them. Julie's Dad added one from his own bed.

"It's damp down here, and I don't want anyone catching cold," he said. Then he and Mrs. Gonner settled in their nest, and the candles were blown out. A kerosene lantern was turned low on the basement stairs.

Iris closed her eyes. It didn't help. The noise from outside was louder than it had been earlier. She heard glass break. Julie turned over, and her parents slept on.

Iris woke with a start! Julie sat up in bed. A terrible crack had woken them. From across the cellar, Iris heard Mr. Gonner say, "Huh!" and he and Mrs. Gonner sat up.

"Wallace! Where was that?"

"I'm going up. Turn up the lantern, and I'll use it."

"Wait 'til morning when you can see," said his wife.

"Elsie, I can't wait. You and the girls light a candle and stay put." He took the bright lantern and went up the stairs. Within minutes, he was back, shaking his head. "The oak between us and the post office fell on our walkway. There's a limb in our dining room. Let's wait 'till morning when we can see. I think the sun's coming up just now."

Iris spoke up, "Oscar can help you chop wood, and Julie and I can clean up glass and twigs." As soon as the words were out of her mouth, Iris knew that the only thing she wanted to do was go home. She wanted to check on her own family and farm house.

Mr. Gonner agreed, "Oscar's a good worker. He and his Dad are golden!"

Iris thought, golden, yes. Oscar is golden.

FEBRUARY

Saturday, February 13th began peacefully. Iris slept late. The sun warmed the foot of her bed. Sleepily, she burrowed under her quilts and listened for sounds in the house. She was glad this was Saturday. The past week of school seemed to last a month. The temperature didn't get above zero. She would never get used to this! Her father said she would. He spent a lot of time in the tractor shed. There was a small wood stove in there. What did he do out there? Sometimes Oscar's Dad would come over, and they'd disappear for hours. There was nothing left to grease or polish on that tractor! She burrowed under the quilts again. Everybody in Harmony was excited about the Andersen baby. Her family could hardly wait until the end of the month, her mother's due date. She hadn't been able to see her feet for months. Neighbors brought food: rhubarb pies, canned green beans, applesauce, bar cookies, and hot dishes. The women at Green Hill Lutheran church had a schedule set up for meals. She could smell a pan of cinnamon rolls heating in the oven. Those were from Mrs. Brenna.

There was someone walking around downstairs, her mother, from the sound of slippers shuffling in the kitchen. She followed her mother in her mind as she went to the sink for water to make coffee, heard her clink the china coffee jar. Then she heard a startled gasp and a weak cry. Next she heard a kitchen chair scrub across the floor and her mother's "uff-da!" as she sat down and then, "Horace," next, a loud, "Ah!"

Iris pulled off the covers, hopped into slippers and tore down the stairs. Her Daddy was coming out of the bedroom and they almost collided at the foot of the stairs. He was dressed for the day.

"Mother?" Iris moved to her mother's side. She sat in her kitchen chair, both hands rubbing her enormous tummy. Uncle Luke was right. She did look like she had a watermelon under her robe.

"Laura Ellen?" Her father kneeled at his wife's side. "I think we're going to have a baby," he said, and smiled at his wife.

"Horace, it's too cold to go to the hospital."

"You know, I put the car in the barn so it won't be too cold. I'm sure it will start first thing."

"I'll get Laughing Sky," offered Iris. "Won't take a minute." She started for the door.

"Wait," called her father, "Get your coat! No need to rush. Babies take a while."

"I'm not sure," said Laura Ellen with a quizzical look on her face. "After three children, I know…"

Iris raced up the stairs and dressed in a jiffy. She grabbed her coat, hat, stuffed her feet into her boots, and headed to the door. The plan was that Laughing Sky would stay with the girls while Horace took their mother to the hospital in Rochester. This had been worked out in detail. Laura Ellen's suitcase was packed and waiting by the door. Each girl had taken a turn choosing what clothes their new brother (or sister) would wear when they returned from the hospital. There was a soft yellow blanket, a white flannel nightgown, and undershirt, and yellow booties crocheted by their mother. A tiny knitted cap Julie's mother had made was also included. It was white, with tiny blue bunnies around the edge.

Before Iris could get out of the door Laura Ellen grabbed her husband's hand and said, "Call Dr. Brenna. I'm not going to the hospital. This baby is on the way."

Iris left as her father picked up the phone to dial the operator. Oh my gosh, she thought. Mama's going to have a baby right here! She banged out the back door.

Iris knocked on Laughing Sky's door and it immediately opened. Laughing Sky stood there, her coat buttoned, and her wool scarf around her neck.

"How did you know?" asked Iris.

"I'm not sure. Let's hurry."

As soon as Iris and Laughing Sky entered the kitchen, Laughing Sky pulled off her coat, gloves, hat, and boots, and hurried into the bedroom. Neither her father nor Laughing Sky said anything to the girls. Martha Rose kicked her feet against her chair. Merry had a piece of paper in front of her. She was drawing snowflakes. Odd sounds came from behind the door. It sounded like their mother was throwing hay bales into the loft. Every now and then their father came out. He looked excited, scared, and worried. Once he got some water from the steaming kettle. Once he gathered towels, then more towels. He would look at the three girls, shake his head, and hurry back into the bedroom.

When the doctor arrived, Laughing Sky was saying, "Yes!" Then there was a weak cry followed by a soft mewing sound. As Dr. Brenna opened the bedroom door, a loud "Wahhh!" filled the air. He hurried in. Iris' father called out, "It's a boy!"

Merry asked, "What's he crying for?"

Martha Rose answered, "He's surprised!"

The three girls jumped up and hugged one another. The door opened again and Dr. Brenna called out, "You might as well come in and say good morning to one impatient baby." Iris' father stood at the foot of the bed holding their new brother, naked, bright pink, wrapped in a soft towel. The baby was a mess. He had black hair, wet and slimy. Laughing Sky leaned across the bed to hug Laura Ellen. They laughed and cried at the same time. Horace raised his new son to his shoulder and patted the baby while tears streamed down his face. "Here's my boy," he said with wonder.

Dr. Brenna spoke up, "You did the easy part." He turned to Laura Ellen, "And how are you?" He smoothed curls hair from the new mother's forehead. Iris was surprised to see that her mother's face was covered with sweat.

"Relieved. Horace, let me have my son." Laura Ellen took the baby in her arms and kissed his cheek. "Oh, he's so tiny. Is he all right? What a lot of black hair he has. Horace, he looks like you!"

"Not with that hair, he doesn't," said Horace. "Look, he has curls."

The baby wiggled one arm out of his covering and waved it in the air.

"He's saying 'hi' to us," laughed Martha Rose. She waved in return, "Hi, Ben!"

Iris thought his little hands looked like star fish.

Dr. Brenna spoke up. "Let us get baby warm, and mother cleaned up. I promise I will bring your brother in the kitchen so you can watch him sleep. Your mother could use some sleep. I bet you were up all night, am I right?"

"I was," said Horace. "My sweet wife here slept more than I did."

"Can he can sleep in my doll cradle?" asked Martha Rose. "He's too big for the other one…"

"Let's put his clothes on," said Merry. "I picked out the yellow booties. Do you think he needs his hat?"

Their mother gave a tired, "Yes. Hat."

When Laughing Sky pulled the yellow night gown over Ben's head, it reached way beyond his feet. The booties hung off his tiny heels.

Martha Rose commented, "Too big! All his clothes are too big!"

Laughing Sky wrapped Ben in a blanket, and carried him into the kitchen.

She carried him to the window and stared out at the horizon. "Look, Benjamin," she said, and turned the baby so he faced the window.

"What do you see?" asked Iris.

Laughing Sky continued to gaze out of the window then turned and wiped her face with one hand.

"What is it?" asked Iris again.

"Brightness touched this house," she said with wonder in her voice.

"Oh, angels," replied Martha Rose. "Ben came with angels."

Merry and Iris slid their eyes towards each other then looked at their little sister and Laughing Sky. Their faces were bright and they grabbed each other in a tight hug.

Martha Rose turned to the table. "I want breakfast! I'm ravishing."

"Martha Rose, you're just plain silly," said Iris. "And,

you're not the baby anymore so you have to use the right words. It's "ravenous," not "ravishing." Ravishing means beautiful."

"Can't I be ravishing and ravenous?" asked the little girl.

"You certainly may," smiled Laughing Sky. "You may be ravenous *and* ravishing and a big sister, all in one day."

Martha Rose pointed to herself, "I'm a big sister all day, and I want a cinnamon roll!"

Horace and the girls stood by the telephone. He dialed PY52238, their Grannie's number in Richmond. Laura Ellen sat up in bed with Benjamin in her arms. He was jerking his arms and making sounds like a puppy. The bedroom door was open so their mother could hear the conversation. Laughing Sky was finishing the dishes. When the phone rang in Richmond and their Grannie answered, the girls yelled together, "It's a boy!"

Their father grinned at the phone. "Yes, Ma'am, you have an impatient grandson. He is tiny, but lively, no bigger than a loaf of bread. Your daughter is the picture of health and so is little Benjamin Patrick. He has a lot of black hair, and eyebrows you could see in the dark. He looks just like his Mama. What? Oh, the girls? They were here for the whole thing. Sat in the kitchen like statues until they heard that cry. Oh, yes, he definitely has your side of the family's hair. I just hope he's as nice as you are. Yes. I will tell her. She knows it but it's nice to hear. Yes, I'll tell the girls also. We love you back. Laura Ellen will call tomorrow with details. Maybe you should make a trip to Minnesota this summer. Yes, yes. We are a lucky family. Goodbye, Mom."

He turned to the waiting faces. "She loves you all, but you knew that."

MARCH

"It smells like a bakery in here." Martha Rose snuggled next to her daddy in the big Oldsmobile. She had grown tall enough so that now, after her fourth birthday, she could see out of the front windshield. She made a point of racing to the car to be sure of her place in the front seat. Iris sat in the back seat holding a basket of bread.

Horace glanced at her in the rear mirror "Do you think we can trust Iris with the bread?" he teased. "That fragrance is mighty tempting!"

Martha Rose twisted around in her seat. "Iris, don't you touch my bread," she warned.

Iris sighed, "Martha Rose, this is not your bread. Mother let you punch it down and knead it a few minutes. I think I can last 'till we get to Miss Catherine's to have a piece."

Horace looked at his youngest daughter. "Your mother did a real job on you this morning," he admired, grinning. "Not a hair out of place, socks that match, shoes shined…"

Martha Rose interrupted. "These are my Sunday shoes." She pointed her toes. "Mother says that old ladies notice everything!"

Her father replied, "Well, Miss Catherine and Miss Alice will have an eyeful when they see you. Merry's coat fits you this winter and that blue matches your eyes. Martha Rose, you look like an angel."

Iris shook her head in the back seat.

Martha Rose spoke up, "Daddy, did you know Miss Catherine's seen an angel? A real one." She spoke in a confidential whisper.

"Is that right?" her father asked in an impressed voice.

"It sumptuously is," said Martha Rose.

From the back seat Iris prompted, "It 'certainly' is. Get it right, Martha Rose."

Her father continued, "Well if anyone could see an angel it would be our Miss Catherine. She's a saint among us. You've been lucky to have her for your Sunday school teacher, Martha Rose."

The three Andersens rode in silence until Horace pulled off the blacktop and onto a dirt driveway that led to a cozy farmhouse tucked into a windbreak of trees.

He spoke up, "Now, we won't out-stay our welcome. Miss Catherine has been very ill and needs her rest."

Martha Rose asked, "Is Miss Catherine going to die?"

"Martha Rose, you know there is one thing we can all count on, and that's dying. Miss Catherine could die any minute. Nobody gets to choose when or how their time on earth will end."

"But nobody can tell stories like Miss Catherine," Martha Rose said with a pout.

Her father smiled. "Maybe with a little help, another person could learn to be a good storyteller. You're a pretty good story teller yourself."

Iris nodded emphatically.

"I know I am," replied her little sister. "Miss Catherine says we're 'two peas in a pod'."

Horace laughed and lifted his hand to ruffle the blonde bangs that lay on his daughter's forehead. "You're so clean this morning you look like you're wearing a halo."

Iris muttered, "Halo?"

"Don't muss my hair, Daddy," instructed Martha Rose.

When the car stopped, Iris saw a face at the kitchen.

"There's Miss Alice," she said and waved.

Martha Rose opened the car door and jumped out. "Look, Iris, there's no snow here."

Her father spoke up, "Don't worry. That doesn't mean a thing. March is not spring. Old Man Winter likes to tease us. March is the snowiest month."

Miss Alice opened the door before Martha Rose could knock. Horace and Iris followed the little girl into the warm house.

"Greetings, greetings," Miss Alice called to them gaily. "Sister is looking forward to seeing you. Oh! Laura Ellen's scrumptious bread. Now, I'm sure that will get Catherine's appetite going. She hardly eats you know, thin as a stick." Miss

Alice paused for breath as she untied her apron strings. "Goodness. You can see that I don't have much company. I don't know when to stop chattering. Welcome, Horace. How is your sweet wife and that baby. I want to hear all about him. Look at Martha Rose! My, oh, my, you are a sight. Pretty as a picture. And this big sister, you're almost a woman, Iris Andersen! Take off your coats and lay them on that chair and you girls run along upstairs and cheer sister. Horace, I'll let you help me with the tea tray." Miss Alice bustled through a doorway with Horace close behind her. Martha Rose and Iris giggled silently at the sight of their tall father following the short plump figure of Miss Alice into the kitchen. Then they went up the polished stairs.

At the top of the stairs a door stood open. Iris looked into the room. Martha Rose pushed past her and called, "Miss Catherine? Are you sleepin' in here?"

Iris saw a tiny lady in bed. She hardly made a lump under the quilt. Martha Rose walked up the side of the bed. Miss Catherine's eyes were closed. "Miss Catherine," the little girl whispered, "Miss Catherine, it's me, Martha Rose Andersen!"

"Oh! Oh, my," said the elderly lady blinking her eyes and trying to focus the blue gaze. "Oh, what a lovely vision to wake to…and Martha Rose, you must always say, 'it is I'." Miss Catherine held out her thin white hand and pointed. "Bring those chairs close to my bed."

Iris pulled two fragile cane-bottomed chairs close to the bed.

Miss Catherine smiled weakly. "You must forgive me. You are Laura Ellen's daughter too. There are so many children…"

"That's Iris, my biggest sister," chirped Martha Rose. "You don't know her because she is too big to be in your class. You know, Miss Catherine, you got a wobbly hand."

Iris exclaimed, "Martha Rose!"

Miss Catherine examined her shaky fingers with surprise. "It's wobbly," she agreed. "You know, when you came in the room, I was 'most gone. I believe you brought me back from the edge of that river." The old lady seemed to sink into her pillow.

71

"Oh, Miss Catherine," breathed Martha Rose.

"Oh, yes," her friend waved her hand. "Quite a few times now I've almost drifted away and here I am...again."

Martha Rose scooted her chair up until her knees touched the bed covers. "You know, my Daddy says you could die any minute. But, Miss Catherine, you've got to be our Sunday School teacher. No one tells stories like you. When you tell that one about the ark, and make those animal noises and act out the storm...."

"Martha Rose," Miss Catherine spoke in a quavering voice, "I won't be telling boys and girls any more stories. Now, that's the truth." The invalid shook her head gently and let out a trembling sigh. "I'm glad you girls came, two angels to see me off."

Iris could hardly take her eyes of the woman. Miss Catherine's face was criss-crossed with wrinkles and her wispy white hair fine as a baby's.

"Well, before you go, Miss Catherine, would you tell my sister one story?" The little girl took her teacher's hand in hers. "You've got cold hands! When my sister, Merry, gets cold hands, I do this." Martha Rose put the cool hand of her friend between her two warm ones. "Now, that's a 'hand sandwich.'" Martha Rose giggled.

Iris poked her with her elbow. "Shhh," she whispered.

Miss Catherine had closed her eyes. He eyelashes were as white as her hair, her eyelids motionless.

"Miss Catherine, are you sleeping?" asked Martha Rose.

"No," the old lady answered. "Resting my eyes. I can hardly see anyway. Thank you for your warm hands. I can feel your pulse."

After a quiet moment, Martha Rose pleaded, "Just one more. Tell the angel story, the one you promised to tell me."

Speaking so softly that Iris had to stand and lean close, Miss Catherine began.

"Once I saw an angel, a magnificent man. He had broad shoulders that widened to form wings. They looked natural like everybody should have a pair. Oh, the sight was more than I could stand. He was bright and shining. I closed my eyes, but like the sun, I knew he was still there." Miss Catherine's faced glowed from remembering. Iris had never seen anyone with such transparent skin. Thin blue veins were visible at Miss Catherine's temples.

"Martha Rose whispered, "Where was he, Miss Catherine?"

"It happened at my father's funeral. The angel stood up in front of church like pillar of gold and blazed away. No one else saw him. It surprised me so that I stopped crying. I was a little girl. Seems like yesterday."

Martha Rose leaned forward "Then what?"

Iris touched her sister on the shoulder and shook her head. "Then, nothing…and everything," said Miss Catherine.

"What does that mean? What did he say?" asked Martha Rose.

The old woman wearily opened her eyes and turned her head. "Say? Angels don't need words." A frown wrinkled Miss Catherine's forehead, and a puzzled look came over her face.

"I'm going to get Daddy," said Iris as the old woman's eyelids began to flutter and fail to open.

"Don't go," said Miss Catherine.

Iris felt a warm hand on her shoulder. "Oh, Daddy," she said, "I think Miss Catherine wants to take a nap." She looked behind her and gasped.

"You!" Miss Catherine looked behind Iris. She had said the word with more strength than Iris thought possible. The old lady's face was bright and her eyes wide open. She began to croon, "A band of angels coming after me, coming for to carry me home." She closed her eyes and her head fell to one side.

Martha Rose looked at her sister and then her friend. Miss Catherine was still.

Iris sat down heavily in the chair. "Martha Rose, did you see that?" Her shoulder was still warm from where the hand had lain.

Martha Rose didn't answer. Her eyes were wide as saucers.

"Here's a lovely tea Sister, and a good-looking man to

visit!" Miss Alice and Iris' father entered the bedroom.

"Daddy!" burst from Iris as she ran and circled his waist with her arms. Horace raised the tray of tea cups over her head and glanced at the still form on the bed. He placed the tray on a nearby table.

Martha Rose looked up at her father. "Look, Daddy. Look out the window."

Iris looked towards the window but her father interrupted. "Miss Alice, I'll go downstairs and call the doctor. Come with me, girls. Miss Alice will want to stay with her sister." He put his hand on Miss Alice's shoulder. "I'm sorry," he said.

"This is what she wanted you know, to slip into sleep. You go on downstairs and use the phone. I'll wait here. I don't want to leave sister alone.

Martha Rose spoke up, "Oh, she's not alone. All these angels came and got her, and she was singing. They made it snow. Look, Daddy." Martha Rose led her father to the window. "They clapped their wings like this," the little girl pushed her arms behind her and waved them. "They made this humming sound. Oh, didn't you hear it?"

Horace and Miss Alice looked at the child's flushed face.

Iris spoke in a calm voice. "One put his hand right here," She touched her shoulder.

Horace spoke in a quiet voice. "Come downstairs with me, girls. "It was the voice he used when he meant business. Both sisters followed him into the hall.

Martha Rose asked, "What took you so long, Daddy?"

"Miss Alice had the tea tray ready. We came up right away. I'm sorry you found Miss Catherine like that."

Iris looked at her father, "Like what, Daddy?"

"Well, gone," he answered.

"Oh, she didn't go anywhere. We had a talk. I so wanted to hear the story about the angel again," said Martha Rose.

Horace knelt in front of his youngest child. "Martha Rose, Miss Catherine was as cold as stone," he began.

"She sure was," agreed the little girl. "I held her hand."

Iris said, "She could hardly keep her eyes open but when

that angel appeared, you should have seen her. He put his hand right here. He did!"

"Yes, and Daddy, she opened her eyes like this." Martha Rose widened her eyes.

Their father stood up. "Girls, your friend has died."

"We know that. We were here when the angels came and the snow. You haven't even looked." Martha Rose's lower lip began to quiver.

Horace went to the window. He could see heavy wet snow falling. He moved closer to the window. A gust of wind blew the snow into a bright spiral, ascending.

APRIL

Dear Journal,
Today is Sunday. Lunch is finished. Merry is sketching chairs at the kitchen table. She's drawn four small rockers, and two straight-back chairs. Martha Rose is asleep on the sofa with Benjamin. Mother is dozing in the kitchen rocker, and Daddy is at Earl and Oscar's house talking about tractors and stuff. It's Sunday in Richmond, too. People went to my church today. The girls and women wore hats and gloves like you're supposed to. Men wore suits and ties. Maybe Dorothy sat with Grandma. I hate to think of Grandma in church without Grandpa. I wore my winter coat this morning—and boots. There is a foot of snow on the ground. I know nobody wore boots at Emmanuel! Grandmother wrote and said that daffodils, azaleas, forsythia and quince are blooming. Just one day there would get me through the rest of the year.
Nobody there knows what it's like here, and nobody here knows what it's like there. Martha Rose is already forgetting. Benjamin will never know. Here I am in this white house surrounded by white fields with no sign of life. I can see smoke from Laughing Sky's chimney, at least that. After lunch in Richmond, people visited. Uncle Paul would come over and play carroms with Daddy on the porch while Aunt B. and mother sat on the glider in the yard drinking iced tea. People walked up and down our street and said, "Hello," to folks sitting on their porches. Sometimes they'd say, "Pretty day, ain't it?" I think that's where Martha Rose picked up "ain't." I sure wish she'd break that habit. It's embarrassing.
Maybe I'll walk over and visit Laughing Sky. I don't know how or why she lives alone. She probably needs company, too. I'm going over.
What did I do when I didn't have a journal to talk to?

Iris gently shook her mother's shoulder. "Mother, I'm bored. I'm going to visit Laughing Sky, Okay?"
Her mother nodded and said, "Mmmmm...." Iris guessed

76

that meant yes.

She opened and closed the back door without waking Cookie who slept soundly at her mother's feet.

Her boots made a trail in the melting snow to Laughing Sky's cabin. Iris could see her at her loom by the front windows. She had recently returned to her loom after breaking her ribs and collar bone. She complained that she got tired and her shoulders were sore. Iris' mother often rubbed them with camphor. When Iris stomped up the stairs, knocking snow off her boots, she had a flash-back of her mother and Laughing Sky crumpled on the ground, and her, frozen in time. She shook the picture from her head and knocked on the door.

Laughing Sky opened the door with a smile on her face. She took Iris by the shoulder and hurried her into the room. "I'm so glad to see you! All I've heard all day is this loom. I need a break. What's going on at the Andersen house this afternoon?"

"Oh, you wouldn't believe it! Everybody is asleep. Daddy went to town to talk about farm stuff with Earl and Oscar, and wouldn't let me go with him. I didn't really want to talk about carburetors anyway, whatever they are. I wrote in my journal, then I saw your chimney smoke, and told myself I'd walk over and see a real live person and ask you questions about growing up. When I came up the steps I remembered you and Mother in a heap at the bottom, and I had to shake my head hard to get that out. Then, there you were at your loom. What are making?"

"Mrs. Gonner asked me to make a shawl for Mrs. Ludvigson."

"Oh, she'll love that color," said Iris. "What do you call it…I think I've talked too much already."

Laughing Sky hugged her young friend, "Oh, I'm so happy you're here. I call this pattern a river, all the blues and greens in my yarn box are in it, and Iris, you may talk all you want, and I'll listen to every word. Sit by the fire and we can keep each other company."

Iris sat in a chair made of birch wood. It had dark red cushions at the back and bottom. There were two chairs like this in front of the fireplace, very cozy.

Before Laughing Sky sat down she took a bundle of paper from a small table, and put them in Iris' lap. "Look, Luke sends letters and poems. I can't imagine how he feels there with Anna, waiting to come here. He's so excited about building a house here. Right now he has to keep up with teaching, writing, and changing diapers."

"Who watches Anna when he's teaching?" asked Iris.

"Oh, Anna is the star of the show everywhere. Luke says his students are lined up asking to stay with her, but he has a woman come from the college. She keeps the English classrooms clean. Luke likes her because she speaks Ojibway with Anna."

"Is she an Indian?" asked Iris.

"Yes, she is."

Iris looked around the room. The fireplace mantle had a kerosene lantern on it.

There were a couple of small tables, and the huge loom. The tiny kitchen had a stove, and a free-standing cupboard where Laughing Sky kept her bread, potatoes, and dishes. Really, there wasn't much in the cabin. "Laughing Sky, what kind of a house are you and Uncle Luke going to build? Will you still come here and weave?"

"Until we get our house built, all three of us will live here. I can't imagine it. Luke says he has bookcases full of books. He built the bookcases, so he'll bring them with him. We're going to be crowded. I can't wait."

"I can't either. Tell me about the wedding. Tell me about the party. Tell me what you are going to wear! Tell me everything. First though, Tell me why you live here by yourself? It seems like last month that Daddy found your cabin in a snow storm and you saved Merry's life, but it's been over a year. I know your grandmother saved a family during the influenza epidemic, and that's how this cabin got built, but why do you live here, and not on the reservation?"

Laughing Sky looked at her hands. She stretched them out in front of her, her long thin fingers supple and brown. "First, I did not save Merry's life. Dr. Brenna gets credit for that." She was silent, looking down at her hands. "My hands look like my mother's. That is all I remember about my mother, her hands. She died when I was two years old."

Iris looked up at her friend. "Like Anna's mother who died when Anna was a baby."

"No." Laughing Sky let her hands fall in her lap and took a deep breath, then said, "Not like Anna's mother, not at all. My mother was murdered."

"Oh, Laughing Sky!" Iris leaped from her seat, the letters and poems spilling onto the floor. "Oh, Laughing Sky," she repeated. Iris moved forward to hug her friend.

Laughing Sky put her hand up to stop her. "Wait. I'm going to tell you. I've told your mother, and I've told Luke. Please, sit. Let me tell it, and it will be done."

Iris sat in her chair. The fire crackled, and the day darkened.

"My grandmother, Wise Eyes, raised me. When One Deer was five-years-old, and I was two, my mother and father were not happy. Another man in our tribe looked at my mother. My mother looked back at him. They spoke words that married people should save for their husbands or wives. My father was angry. He took my mother on a fishing trip. He insisted she go with him. He drowned her. He was sent away. His name is never spoken, nor my mother's. Grandmother brought my brother and me here to get us away from the stares of the tribe. We would stay for a month or more. When Grandmother died, One Deer brought me here to stay. I was sixteen; he was nineteen.

I have been here most of the last five years. He travels to the Red Lake reservation, and to Canada to work on tribal councils. I'm used to being alone now. Dr. Brenna and his wife have been like family to me. They sell my blankets and weavings, and he teaches me his medicine, while I teach him the Indian way. We work well together. Right now, I feel well-loved. That is a good feeling. I have you and your family, Luke, the people in this town, and Anna. I couldn't ask for anything more."

After she spoke, silence deepened in the room. Iris thought she knew her friend, but she had no idea what her life had been. No wonder Laughing Sky was close to Iris' mother. Other than One Deer, Iris' family was the only family she had. When Uncle Luke married her, she truly would be family, Iris' family.

Iris couldn't think of one word to say. She looked at her friend. She looked around the sparsely furnished cabin. It was perfect that Anna would have Laughing Sky for a mother. No matter how awful it was that the little girl's parents had died, she would be loved like no other little girl Iris could imagine.

Laughing Sky took a deep breath. "You know my story. One Deer is my brother, and soon will be yours. Your Uncle Luke, Anna and I are going to be happy together. Wise Eyes will be smiling."

The two of them sat in silence. Laughing Sky's head was bowed, her hands motionless in her lap. Iris stood up. She put one hand on her friend's good shoulder, then left.

It took Iris a long time to get home. She walked slower and slower until she stopped on the path. She thought: compare my childhood to Laughing Sky's. Then came questions: How did I get so lucky? How does a person continue after a tragedy like her friend's? How would I have survived if my mother had been murdered? How could anybody? No one deserves that life.

Iris began to walk again. Then, she ran. Her house waited for her. In it was her mother, father, sisters and brother. There was a dog, two cats, two horses and a sheep in the barn. It was all in front of her. Out of breath, tears running down her face, she opened the kitchen door. Her mother stood, smoothing the table cloth. Her sisters were at the table buttering their toast. For one second, the scene in front of her froze. Then, the spell broke. Iris grabbed her mother by her shoulders, buried her head in her sweet neck, and wept. Her mother patted her on the back and began to croon, "Oh, Iris, my big girl, hush, hush. Be still. Take a deep breath. We're here. We're all together." She pushed Iris' hair behind her ears. Iris calmed, and sagged into her chair.

Martha Rose looked at her big sister and said, "Eat this." She pushed her plate of pancakes Iris' way. "I always feel better when I eat pancakes."

MAY

One more week of school, and Iris would be free to spend the day in the woods near the stream with Merry, Martha Rose and Cookie. Maybe even Ben!

She'd read all afternoon, ride War Bonnet with Oscar and Blue, write in her journal, and get ready for the wedding. What she looked forward to most was spending time with Julie and Oscar. Of course, Oscar. Oscar and his father came to dinner about once a month. Sometimes she saw him in town when she went with her father. Sometimes he rode out to see what was happening on the farm. Maybe he came to see her? Maybe he came to see Martha Rose and Ben. Iris loved the way he played with her brother. To see a boy playing with a baby the way he did was unusual. She didn't remember boys in Richmond paying attention to any baby. Oscar was comfortable with Ben. Ben would pat his face, grab his nose, and say, "Ahh!" Oscar would say, "He's trying to say my name!" Iris would remind him that Benjamin was four months old and not ready to talk. "He knows me," Oscar would add. Her mother agreed.

Late in the month, Oscar and his Dad came for dinner on Saturday. As soon as the meal was done, Martha Rose took Oscar by the hand and said, "Come with me! Iris, you come, too."

Merry asked, "What about me?"

"No," replied her little sister. "You would be too many."

"I'm not playing with you tomorrow," said Merry, turning away. I'm going to use your crayons, too."

"Fine," said her little sister.

Martha Rose led Oscar and Iris out of the back door, and around the side of the house. "On the first day I lived here, I told Daddy I would find a segret cubby for me, an' I looked and looked, and I found it." Martha Rose stood in the front yard facing the house. "There," she pointed at a group of tall shrubs at the corner of the house under the living room window. "Can you see it?"

Iris asked, "What are we looking for?"

Martha Rose grinned. "Oscar, can you see it?"

He replied, "I see bushes."

"Well, look here," Martha Rose walked up to the shrubs, pulled a branch aside, and disappeared. "Come in," she called.

Oscar looked at Iris, shrugged his shoulders, took her hand and said, "Come on!"

When Iris walked under the branches and looked in, she realized she was standing in the middle of a clear circle. The shrubbery had originally been planted in a circle, and overgrown its boundaries. Martha Rose had found a secret place all right. No one could see her. She had brought a small rug from the kitchen.

"Sit down," Martha Rose instructed.

Iris and Oscar sat on the rug. Iris drew her hand away. Martha Rose stood over them.

"Now. This is my segret cubby. Don't tell Merry. Don't tell Daddy. Don't tell Mommy. Oscar, don't you tell your Daddy."

"What are you going to do out here?" asked Oscar.

"I'm gonna hide," said Martha Rose.

"Why would you hide?" he asked.

"So nobody can find me."

Iris looked up at her sister. Martha Rose had a mean look on her face. She said, "Martha Rose, you've never hidden from anybody. You like people more than anybody I know. Who are you hiding from?"

"I can't tell."

"You let us know about your secret place. You can tell us," said Iris.

Martha Rose crossed her arms over her middle. "Can't. She might find out."

"She?" Iris and Oscar asked together.

Martha Rose shook her finger at Iris and Oscar. "She said she'd come to my house and get me good! She's big and she could do it!"

"Martha Rose, everybody in Harmony loves you. You're everybody's favorite little girl," said Oscar, "including mine."

"Well, one person don't like me and she's big. She thinks

she is gonna' get me but she won't find me!"

Oscar and Iris looked at each other. Who in the world had Martha Rose made mad enough to threaten her?

Iris said, "Martha Rose, Oscar and I will never give away your secret. When I can't find you, I'll know you are out here safe. You don't need to tell Oscar and me but you do need to tell Mother about the girl who threatened you."

"Ain't a girl."

"You said, 'she'," said Iris.

"Ain't a girl. It's a old woman."

"Martha Rose, Let's go in. It's going to get dark. I don't want you to be here in the dark," said Iris.

"If she comes in the dark, I'm gonna' come out here in the dark," insisted Martha Rose.

Oscar got up, pushed the branches away for the girls, and said, "When does she come here?"

"Only one time. She scared me and said she'd come back and get me."

"Martha Rose, can you tell me when she came?" Iris asked.

"She came on two days ago," answered Martha Rose.

Iris' eyes went wide. She took Martha Rose's hand, grabbed Oscar's hand, and ran for the house. As soon as the three of them were in the kitchen, Iris, still holding Martha Rose by the hand, walked up to her mother. Her mother sat in the kitchen rocker, Ben asleep in her lap. Oscar's Dad sat nearby, his harmonica in his hand. It appeared that he had played little Ben to sleep.

"Mother," Iris began. "Martha Rose and I need to talk to you right now."

Oscar spoke up, "Let me hold Benjamin."

One look at Iris' face and her Mother carefully transferred the baby to Oscar's arms. He took her place in the rocker, cuddling the baby.

"Let's go into my room," her mother said.

Martha Rose pulled back on Iris' hand. "You said you wouldn't tell. Now you're telling and I'm not goin' in dere!"

Iris closed the door to her Mother and Father's bedroom. She continued to hang onto Martha Rose. "Mother, Martha Rose needs to tell you something. It's important."

Martha Rose stood still, her eyes clenched shut, her mouth tight in a straight line.

"What is it? Martha Rose, talk to me." Iris' mother held out her hand to her youngest girl and pulled her over to the bed to sit next to her. Martha Rose would not sit down. She stood by the bed.

"I am not tellin'. Iris, I will never tell you a segret." Martha Rose had her arms crossed over her chest. "Never!"

Iris began, "Martha Rose, this is important. It's not right for anyone to threaten you anywhere!"

"Threaten?" her mother asked.

"Oh, you," said Martha Rose with a stamp. She turned to her mother. "Dat lady who comed here two days before today told me she was going to come back and get me good!"

"What did this lady look like?" asked her mother.

"She was old and big and had a hat like this." Martha Rose swirled her hand over her head.

"Oh! Oh!" began Iris' Mother. Then she began to smile. She tried to hide her face between her hands, but soon, she was giggling, then laughing. "Oh, Martha Rose! That was Mrs. Ludvigson! She writes books. She loves children. She has a colorful way of talking. I'm sure she meant she looked forward to seeing you again. She and I had a good talk. She's starting a book reading group."

"No. She said she was gonna get me good!"

"I will invite her to visit tomorrow. We'll straighten this out, don't you worry."

"I won't be here," said the little girl.

The next day Mrs. Ludvigson did come to the Andersen farm. She was dressed in turquoise, Iris' favorite color. She carried a bulging cloth bag, and a wide-brimmed straw hat. Martha Rose was nowhere to be seen. Iris' Mother called from the back porch and the front porch but there was no answer. She looked at Iris, "Do you know where your little sister is?"

"I do."

"Would you please take Mrs. Ludvigson to her?"

Iris looked at the tall red-haired woman next to her Mother. She had the kindest face Iris had ever seen, calm blue eyes, and a small pink mouth.

"I've brought books to share with your sister," she said, patting her cloth bag. "I'd like to read one to her."

"I'll take you to Martha Rose but you'll need a chair." Iris picked up a kitchen chair, led Mrs. Ludvigson towards the shrubbery circle in the front yard, then called out, "Martha Rose, you've got company." She walked away but not before she saw Mrs. Ludvigson maneuver her chair and bag of books into Martha Rose's secret cubby.

Iris did not stay and listen. She walked into the house and sat in a kitchen chair.

"Mother, what do you think they are doing?"

Her Mother answered, "Martha Rose didn't understand what Mrs. Ludvigson actually said when she was here. What she said was, 'I am going to come back and set you straight.' She meant that she wants to help Martha Rose with her speech."

"Her speech?"

"We've kept Martha Rose our baby too long. She'll go to school next year, and she can't be saying 'ain't'!"

"Oh, Mother, I love her baby talk. Does she have to go to school? I can hardly bear the thought."

"Iris, oh, Iris. Imagine how I feel." Her mother sighed.

An hour went by. Iris and her Mother didn't do anything. Ben slept in Oscar's arms, Merry drew cats in her room. Her father was in the field kicking dirt clods with Earl Runs Like Fox, and Martha Rose and Mrs. Ludvigson were in the shrubbery.

Suddenly, Martha Rose burst in the back door. "The Hat Lady is gonna' teach me not to say 'ain't' any more. I—am—not. That is what I am gonna say. Martha Rose shook her finger at each syllable of I—am—not. An' she's teachin' me to read an' she can tell stories, an' I finish 'em. I'm gonna be her friend!" She did a little twirl.

Mrs. Ludvigson walked into the kitchen adjusting her book bag. Iris had never seen so much turquoise. Mrs. Ludvigson had put on her hat. This one was beautiful with a wide brim. She was definitely The Hat Lady.

"What a beautiful child you have, Laura Ellen. Martha Rose is ready to read and bursting at the seams to learn. We are going to have a wonderful time. What an imagination! Oh, I must get home to feed my cats. When I neglect them, they let me know it, whining and mewing like I've been gone days. No, I can't stay for tea or anything." The Hat Lady patted Martha Rose on the head. "Oh, I wish I could twirl like you do."

"I'll teach you. I will. You teach me to read and I teach you to twirl!"

"I'd like that. See you in church."

Mrs. Ludvigson waved her gloves in the air. She always had a pair of gloves. Iris had never met anyone like her.

"Mother, where does she get those hats? She takes up two seats in church!" Iris laughed.

"She goes up to St. Paul. Imagine traveling all that way for a hat," said her mother. "I've never been to St. Paul. To people here, you'd think it was the center of the Universe."

"Where's her husband?" asked Iris. "Is she old? With all those hats, I can't tell."

"No, Lois is not old. Lois will never be old. She lives by herself. Her husband died young, very sick for years. We never knew him, but he is quite alive in her life."

"What do you mean?" asked Iris. "Does she talk to him?"

"Not out loud, but she gets a look about her, and I know, I mean, know, he's with her."

Martha Rose went outside. "I'm going back to my cubby," she called.

"Fine, honey," answered her mother.

"Mother," Iris began, then waited until her mother turned and looked at her. "Mother, why does God let people like Mrs. Ludvigson be lonely?" She waited a minute, then screwed up her face and asked, "Why would God ever let Anna's Mother and Father die, and why, why, why, did He let Laughing Sky grow up without a mother or a father? Just wondering about God."

"Oh, my goodness, Iris. What hard questions." She took Iris' hands in her own. Iris remembered that Laughing Sky had said that the only thing she remembered about her mother was her hands. She looked at her mother's hands and her own. Yes. They had similar long fingers.

Then Iris said, "Look Mother, our hands are the same."

Tears filled Laura Ellen's eyes, "Yes, they are. Iris, I thank you for these hard questions. I need to hear them. I'll try to answer, but I only have my answers. You might get a different answer from everyone you ask."

"I don't want to ask anybody else," said Iris.

"I believe," her mother began, then sighed, and began again. "I believe that we are presented with hard things in life, so we will know just how much love there is in the world. When Laughing Sky's mother died, and her father was sent away, One Deer and her grandmother loved her more. Now, here she is, and look at all the people who love her. Mrs. Ludvigson remembers how she was loved by her husband, and that love never lessens. Anna? All Anna knows is love, yours, Oscar's, ours. The whole town of Harmony loves that baby! God is love, Iris. That's my answer. We have terribly hard moments in our life, and if we look, love is there. Now, hug me, I'm going to cry."

Mrs. Ludvigson came to the Andersen farm every Tuesday after lunch. Iris watched as she and Martha Rose disappeared into the shrubbery for an hour, then they twirled out together. When it rained, the two of them spent an hour in in the living room. Mrs. Ludvigson was right. Martha Rose could read, and was learning to spell.

JUNE

Iris sat up, pushed the coverlet off her bed, stood by the side of it, and stretched. Today she would be a bridesmaid! She would wear a pale lavender dotted swiss dress with a white satin ribbon around her waist. She would wear white socks and shiny white shoes. She would carry pink and white peonies in her arms. Merry would wear a blue dotted-swiss dress just like Iris' only, blue, and Martha Rose, the flower-girl, would wear pink. Her mother, Maid of Honor, would wear a white dotted-swiss blouse, and light blue linen skirt. All the girls, including Laughing Sky, would carry peonies from their garden. One Deer would give his sister away, and Horace would be the best man. Luke would carry Anna in his arms.

No one knew what the bride would wear. It wasn't fair! Iris imagined her in a white deer-skin dress with beads clicking as she walked down the garden path to where Pastor Nilsen would stand. The congregation would sing, "Now Thank We All Our God," as the bride and her brother came down the path together, and "Amazing Grace," as Laughing Sky, Luke, and Anna walked back down it again, a family at last.

Iris hurried downstairs and found a bustle of women in the kitchen. Mrs. Nilsen had made a Kransekaka. Iris had never seen one, but she was told it's a tower of baked almond paste circles, and there were lemon bars from Julie's mother, Dr. Brenna was bringing two baked hams. Iris' mother had baked rolls for three days and made enough potato salad to fill a farm wagon. Earl had supplied the potatoes. Iris, Merry, and Oscar had helped scrub, peel and cut them into small pieces.

Laughing Sky and Laura Ellen had spent several afternoons alone in the little cabin across the meadow. Something was up. Iris couldn't stand it when people had secrets. She couldn't keep her own secrets, and when other people could, it got the best of her.

She found her mother leaning into the oven checking on the rolls. "Mother, when will we see Laughing Sky?" asked Iris.

"The bride doesn't appear until she walks down the path,"

answered her mother.

"Just tell me what she's going to wear! I can't stand it. Why shouldn't I know? We're best friends."

"You'll soon see," answered her mother.

"Just give me a hint. Is it an Indian dress?"

"Iris, if you don't leave me alone I'm going to give you a job. In fact, take Ben from Mrs. Brenna, and give that woman a break. Here, give him a roll."

Iris sighed and went over to the kitchen rocker where Mrs. Brenna was playing with Ben. Her little brother reached for the roll and stuffed it in his mouth. He didn't eat rolls. He gummed them until they were soggy. Once he had his roll in his mouth he lifted his arms to his sister and she picked him up.

Mrs. Brenna rose from the chair, "Iris, take my place. I'm going over to help Laughing Sky get dressed."

"Already?" asked Iris.

"Oh, yes. I'll take her a little something to eat and calm her nerves. The getting dressed part is the most fun. It does take some time."

Horace, Luke, Earl, and Oscar were setting up tables from church under the apple trees. As soon as they were up, out came the women with white table cloths from church, vases of lilacs, peonies, and every bowl and platter in Harmony. There were candles on each table, and Iris wondered if the wind would blow them out. Right now, it wasn't windy, but in an hour...

Pastor Nilsen drove up in his Ford, and Mrs Nilsen got out carefully. She had the Kransekaka on a cut-glass platter and made a big show of carrying it to the empty table reserved for it. Pastor brought over some more platters of small bars of the baked almond paste with squiggles of icing. White dish towels were flung over all the food.

Iris was glad the mosquitoes weren't bad. There hadn't been a lot of rain.

"Iris, find your sisters, help them dress, and get them downstairs. Hand Ben over to Mrs. Halker. Your sisters can put on their shoes just before they walk out. I can see those white shoes now when they get out in that yard! Come down and I'll tie your sashes. I have to get dressed, too." Her mother flung her apron over a chair. "This kitchen will never be the same."

Women were taking off their aprons and pushing back strands of hair which had escaped from pins and combs. Mrs. Nilsen smoothed her gray silk dress, and muttered to herself, "I didn't know I'd have an occasion to wear this again." She saw Iris listening and laughed, "Don't worry, Iris, sometimes I am the only person I have to talk to."

Her father came in the door in a hurry. "Earl and Oscar went home to dress. I better make sure Luke knows what time it is. Has anybody seen Luke?"

Iris thought a minute. It wasn't only Luke that was missing. Where was Anna? She had to get dressed too. Iris' mother had made a white lace gown and slip for her.

Her mother stuck her head out of her bedroom door. "Iris! Your sisters!"

If Luke wasn't here, he must be at Laughing Sky's, yet the groom wasn't supposed to see the bride until…Iris sneaked out of the kitchen. Her feet seemed to carry her along, and before she knew, she was at Laughing Sky's cabin. She stepped up on the porch. She could see Mrs. Nilsen standing in front of the bride with a brush in her hand. No sign of Luke or Anna.

Iris ran to the farm house, passed it, and ran into the barn, shutting the double doors behind her. Silence. Joshua, Blue, and War Bonnet shuffled their feet. Snowball was napping in his small pen. This was serious.

She heard people in the yard calling, "Luke! Luke!"

She ran to the house. She better check on her sisters. She could at least do that. She opened the door to Martha Rose's room. Her little sister put her finger to her lips, and Merry pointed to the bed. There lay Luke with Anna curled up next to him, sound asleep. The little girls were giggling.

Merry whispered, "They fell asleep! They don't even know they're going to get married."

Iris touched her uncle's shoulder. "Uncle Luke. Wake up!"

He pulled Anna close to him and snuffled, "Huh?"

Martha Rose spoke up, "Get up, and get married."

Luke looked up and saw the three girls staring at him. "What? Oh, Anna! We've got to get dressed. Look at me."

Luke had on work pants and a shaggy shirt. His hair stood up in spikes. He looked like he was eight years old.

An hour later Iris drifted into another world. Most of the town of Harmony was in her yard dressed in clothes she never would have thought they owned. Everybody was beautiful. Mrs. Ludvigson looked like a bride. Her white straw hat had a tulle veil that covered her face. Her white gloves were sparkling. The men wore suits. Oscar had on a tie and real shoes. His hair was combed to the side, and it made him look like a new Oscar. Iris liked the look. Martha Rose spread the white rose petals, her mother had a pink face, her father looked taller than he'd ever looked to her before, and Laughing Sky! Laughing Sky had on the wedding dress Iris had found in the attic a year ago. She was wearing Iris' grandmother's wedding gown and looked like a princess. She wore a white lace veil over her black hair. Both streamed down her back. Luke had a peony stuck in his lapel and couldn't stop grinning. Hankies came out when Pastor Nilsen asked, "Who gives this woman…" and One Deer croaked, "I do." From then on it was bedlam. The calm farmers and store owners of Harmony clapped, laughed, cried, and hugged each other for the rest of the service.

At the garden party, Anna and Ben were the stars of the show. Ben made a face when he tasted a lemon bar and tears came to his blue eyes. Ten-month-old Anna wiggled and squirmed in every one's arms until One Deer put her down on the grass where she laid on her back, took off her booties, and put her feet in her mouth. What Iris will never forget is how Uncle Luke and Laughing Sky never let go of each other's hands. Not for the wedding or the rest of the day. As the light faded they walked the path to their cabin, still holding hands, Anna slept in the crook of Luke's left arm, his right arm around his new wife.

Iris looked up at the sky. The stars were coming out. Looked like they were close enough to touch. She knew she couldn't but reached her hand up to them anyway. It was that kind of night.

JULY

Iris complained, "It's as hot here as it was in Virginia!" She wiped her forehead on her sleeve. "You can see the heat rising off the road." She placed a glossy ear of corn in a pot, and reached for another ear to shuck.

Laura Ellen sat with a pan of beans on the kitchen table and a pile of shells in her lap. "I wish we would get some rain. These beans won't produce in a hot dry spell." She tilted her head, listening, and turned to Martha Rose, "I think I hear your brother waking up. Would you please entertain him for a few minutes while I finish shelling these beans? I won't be long."

Martha Rose sat fanning herself with a paper accordion-pleated fan she had made in Sunday school. Without getting up, she said, "He's hot. He'll go back to sleep."

Her mother said, "Martha Rose, we are all hot. Now, please, run upstairs and talk to Benjamin for me."

Iris watched her little sister's mouth flatten into a stubborn line.

"I don't want to. May Rhoades said that she was going to tell her mother to take me to the lake with her today."

Laura Ellen looked impatiently at her youngest daughter. "Martha Rose, I have gotten no cooperation from you since the wedding. You aren't going anywhere today. You finish shelling these beans." She got up and walked angrily up the stairs as Benjamin's cries began in earnest.

Iris looked at her little sister. "You're stuck now. Martha Rose, you bring trouble on yourself."

Martha Rose sniffed and picked up a green bean. "I don't care anyway. May's brudders tease us."

Iris saw her little sister's lower lip began to tremble and she sighed, "Oh, Martha Rose."

The telephone rang. Laura Ellen called from upstairs. "Iris, answer that. If it's Mrs. Rhoades tell her Martha Rose isn't going anywhere because she's been uncooperative. Thank her for the offer."

Iris answered the phone and May asked to speak to Martha

Rose. Iris told her that her little sister was in trouble for talking back to her mother, and would not be able to swim. May hung up without saying goodbye.

Iris said, "Your friend needs to learn some phone manners. She's too old to hang up on people."

"She's six," replied Martha Rose.

"Well, that's old enough. If she's old enough to call, she should be old enough to be polite." Iris looked at her sister. "Is she really six? She's tiny."

Laura Ellen called May a "Tom Boy." Her hair was always mussed. May's mother had her hands full with three older boys, and a new set of twins.

Iris and Julie planned to meet at Mrs. Nielsen's house to help her make strawberry jam. She said she could use a couple pair of hands. Merry had gone to a friend's for lunch. Martha Rose was going to be lonely!

Iris and Julie worked beside Mrs. Nilsen in her pale yellow kitchen. Big pots of strawberries and sugar bubbled and boiled while the girls stirred with long wooden spoons to keep the jam from burning. Mrs. Nilsen watched a large kettle boil. It held heavy glass jars they would sterilize for canning. The kitchen was steamy.

Pastor Nilsen stood in the doorway and watched the activity. He smiled and said, "Could a country parson beg a glass of cool water in the midst of this beehive of activity? I don't want to get in the way."

"Well," Mrs. Nilsen defended herself, "If I had let these strawberries sit one more day in this heat, they would have been ruined."

The telephone in the hall rang, and Pastor left to answer it murmuring, "Oh, another compliment on my sermon!" The girls laughed.

Mrs. Nilsen took a turn stirring each pot, and said, "I believe we have reached the point where we can put the jam in the jars." She laid a tea towel on her kitchen table and began to take the hot jars out of the boiling water with tongs. She handed Iris the tongs, and said, "Fish the funnel out of the water for me."

Iris took the large steel funnel out of the boiling water, and placed it in the mouth of one of the hot jars. When she looked up she saw Pastor Nilsen in the doorway. He wasn't smiling.

His wife glanced up and went immediately to his side. "What is it?" she asked.

Pastor Nilsen's face was frozen in a mixture of disbelief and fear. "That was the Sheriff. The Rhoades family, except John's wife and the two babies, went to Goose Lake today, and it seems May disappeared from the group."

Mrs. Nilsen asked, "How long has she been gone?"

Pastor Nilsen took his glasses off and put them in his shirt pocket. He rubbed the indentations on his nose. "She's been gone three hours."

Iris spoke up, "Maybe she decided to walk home…"

Julie added, "Yes, and maybe she got lost."

Mrs. Nilsen looked at the clean jars and pots of strawberries then at her husband's concerned face. "Let's go. We'll drop the girls at their houses and you can take me to the Rhoades' farm."

She put a clean dish towel over the jar, and covered the strawberry pots with lids. She spoke to both girls, "I'm sorry we have to end abruptly. Mrs. Rhoades must be worried to distraction at the farm. I'll go see what I can do. Her big boys will need dinner at least." Thinking aloud she wondered, "What can I bring?" She took a loaf of bread she had received from a church member that morning, and wrapped it in waxed paper, then got a jar of rhubarb sauce from the pantry. She took her apron off and laid it over a chair. "I'm ready," she called to her husband.

Julie and Iris walked silently to the car and got into the back seat. Julie asked, "Can May swim?"

Iris answered, "I doubt it."

~

At the Andersen farm, Iris got out of the car and Pastor Nilsen went with her to find her father. Laura Ellen came out of the house. "My, I'm surprised to see you so soon," she began, and then said, "Iris, what is it?"

Pastor Nilsen asked, "Could I speak to Horace?" He nodded to his car. "Talk to my wife. She has news."

Laura Ellen said, "Horace is in the barn," and walked quickly to the Pastor's car.

Iris went into the house and slumped in a kitchen chair.

Martha Rose turned away from the sink. "Are you sick?" she asked.

Iris sat and looked at her little sister. Martha Rose held a brimming glass of water in her hand. Her bangs were damp and sticking to her forehead.

"It's too too too hot! Do you want water?"

When there was no answer, she added, "Are you mad at me, too?"

Iris jumped from her chair and embraced her sister. The glass of water spilled down her back as she clung to Martha Rose, rocking her from side to side.

Laura Ellen came into the house and shut the screen door carefully. She leaned against the kitchen wall and took a deep breath.

Martha Rose's voice quivered as she asked, "What's wrong?"

Laura Ellen walked to her two girls and took Iris' arms from around her sister. She picked Martha Rose up and sat with her in the big kitchen rocker near the stove. Martha Rose began to pat her mother on the shoulder. "It's all right. It's gona' be all right."

Laura Ellen held out one arm, "Come here, Iris."

Iris sat on the floor next to her mother's chair.

Her mother began, "Martha Rose, Pastor Nilsen and your father have gone to Goose Lake. The Sheriff called Pastor Nilsen and asked for volunteers to find a missing child."

Martha Rose sniffed "I was 'posed to go to Goose Lake with May."

Her mother interrupted her, "Martha, May is the child who is lost."

After a moment of silence the little girl asked, "Where'd she go, Mama?"

Then she looked at Iris sitting on the floor with her arms around her knees, her head bowed. Martha Rose jumped out of her mother's arms. "Don't worry about May! She's playing hide and seek with her brudders. That's all!"

The hazy summer light turned the cornfield golden in the sunset. Iris, Merry, Martha Rose, and their mother sat down to a dinner of potato salad, cold chicken and rolls left over from Sunday dinner. Laura Ellen said, "Let's say grace," and they joined hands and bowed their heads.

Horace came home long after Martha Rose and Merry were in bed. Laura Ellen had decided to rearrange the kitchen cupboards, so she and Iris had stacked all the dishes on the table and counter. Iris was washing the cupboards with warm soapy water. Her mother had said, "It's best to stay busy."

As soon as her father came in the door, he said, "We haven't found her. There's no moon tonight. We'll start again at dawn."

Iris sat down. "Oh, Daddy! What do you think happened?"

Laura Ellen poured a cup of coffee for her husband and pulled out his chair at the table. She pushed a pile of dishes away to make space for his dinner plate which she took out of the oven.

Horace washed his hands and dried them on the towel his wife handed him. He smiled at his wife and kissed her damp forehead before he sat down. "Um, I was hungry and didn't know it!"

Iris asked impatiently, "Daddy?"

He put his fork down. "It doesn't look good. All the children were in the water. They had a "buddy" system. May's buddy, her oldest brother Timothy, said she was with him one minute and the next, she was gone."

Laura Ellen sighed, "Oh, he must feel awful!"

Horace said, "That's not the worst of it. Mrs. Rhoades is blaming her husband for not keeping an eye on May."

"Oh, that won't help," his wife said.

"No one will sleep at that house tonight," he said.

Iris asked, "Do you think she could be lost? Maybe she got in the cornfield and can't find her way out. Mrs. Nilsen said that happens."

Her father shook his head. "We combed that cornfield three times. People got in cars and drove over every road in the county. We made a good search on land and a good one in the water." He shook his head and pushed his plate away "I guess I'm not hungry."

Iris asked, "Can May swim?"

He looked her straight in the eye, "No."

Iris went up to her bedroom. Martha Rose had crawled into her bed and was asleep there, her rear end in the air, rocking back and forth. Iris got in next to her and the little girl turned on her side, fitting snugly into her big sister's arms. Iris lay awake until the birds began to sing and dawn brightened the windows.

When Iris woke, Martha Rose was gone. She yawned, and froze mid-stretch. She dressed and ran barefooted down the steps.

Her mother looked up from the rocker where she was feeding Benjamin. She answered Iris' questioning glance. "Your father left to go to the lake."

"Where's Martha Rose?"

"In the yard throwing sticks for Cookie. Eat a muffin."

"I'm not hungry. I'll eat a plum."

Her mother raised Benjamin to her shoulder and began to pat his back. His head was upright and steady, and he looked at Iris with a serious face. She knelt next to him, "Good morning, little bear, good morning!"

Benjamin burped and blew a bubble.

"Very Good!" Iris applauded. "I don't know anyone whose

little brother can burp and bubble at the same time."

Benjamin's head began to wobble and sink to his mother's shoulder. He struggled to keep his eyes open, but his full tummy and his mother's warm arms won the battle.

Iris looked at the clock and whispered, "It's ten o'clock." She looked out the window and saw Cookie running towards the house with a stick in her mouth, then she dropped the stick and ran down the drive, barking. A car came up the road. In slow motion, Iris set her glass of milk on the counter and went to the back door. Her father got out of the car. Martha Rose ran to her Daddy, and he picked her up in his arms, held her close and came into the house.

Iris' mother came down the steps and stood in the doorway.

Her husband said, "Where's Merry? We'll hear this together."

Martha Rose asked, "Daddy, did you find May? Where did she sleep last night? I waked up and thought she was in our house!"

Merry came in from the living room where she had been drawing the cats.

Horace sat Martha Rose down, put his hands in his pockets, took them out, and leaned on the wooden table. "Some of the men found May this morning tangled in the weeds at the opposite end of the lake." He looked at Martha Rose. "I'm sorry as I can be, honey, but your friend has drowned."

Martha Rose looked up at him. "Does that mean dead?"

"It does."

"And she's not coming back?"

"That's right. She's not coming back."

"I didn't know little girls could die, Daddy."

Laura Ellen took Martha Rose and held her close. She carried her to the rocker and sat with her while the little girl began to cry, first sniffs, then gulps, then noisy sobs.

Iris took Merry by the hand. "Let's go to the barn. We can say anything to Joshua, and he'll listen."

As they crossed the yard, Iris wondered what the old horse had heard in the past. This must be the worst.

AUGUST

This year, 1939, the Harmony Family Picnic would be held in the church yard of Greenfield Lutheran church. Iris sat at a table covered with a white cloth, waiting for other families to arrive. Her mother was always early. When Iris thought back to last year's picnic, she felt weak. What a picnic; her father was in a wheelchair, head bandaged, leg broken. Martha Rose had a sprained ankle, and Iris had a secret. Also, May Rhoades had been there. Her death hung over Harmony like a curtain. At times the curtain would blow open, and the children played and laughed. Without warning, it closed again, and there was silence. Last year, her parents had told her before the picnic that they would leave Harmony. Her Daddy would return to teach English in Richmond, Virginia, in October. Their first year in Harmony tornadoes had destroyed crops. Last year, her father couldn't harvest because he couldn't walk, and certainly couldn't get up in a tractor. He said they weren't meant to farm. Her sisters had no idea they were going back.

That was a year ago? Could it be that in one year Uncle Luke had adopted an Ojibway daughter, and married Laughing Sky? Iris and she were close as sisters. She called her Aunt Laughing Sky.

There had been other calamities. Iris had broken her little finger falling through a window in the library at school, she'd had nightmares that she woke from screaming. Her mother had broken her wrist, Laughing Sky, her collarbone and ribs, and Miss Catherine and May had died. And, she, Iris Andersen, had killed two wolves with a pitch fork. She now had a baby brother. All this in one year? Now, here they were eating potato salad, corn, ham, fried chicken, deviled eggs, jello, and bar cookies in the yard of her church.

Iris thought August was the most important month of the year. Her family left Virginia in August, arrived in Harmony, Minnesota in August, decided NOT to leave Harmony the following August, and now, they were still here, surrounded by friends who didn't look, talk, or act at all like her friends back home. Where was home? She would ask everybody! Iris noticed Mrs. Ludvigson. (You couldn't miss her.) She had on a straw hat with a turquoise scarf that fluttered from its crown. Her dress was grass green and rippled around her legs in the breeze. Mrs. Ludvigson would know about home. Iris would ask her. No, she'd ask Luke first. He had left home, and come back. He'd know. Next she'd ask Oscar. No, maybe she wouldn't. Oscar might get sad thinking about his Mother. Oh, she'd ask him anyway. She liked talking to him better than anybody in Harmony.

Iris looked for Uncle Luke. All of Harmony was here. She knew everybody's names, where they lived, and not just the Lutherans. She knew Methodists and Catholics.

She knew more people here than she had in Richmond. Still, they weren't "her people."

A girl from the High School worked at the pharmacy. If Iris went in alone she'd call out, "Hi, honey," in a fake Southern accent. Oscar said not to let it bother her, but it did. Mrs. Vollum, her teacher this year, said she loved to hear Iris read in class. "Every syllable is beautiful. The class listens to you in a way they don't listen to anybody else. Iris, maybe you are meant for the stage." Uncle Luke thought she was meant, "for the page." She'd been making up stories and writing all summer. When she would bring one to him, he'd hold it up and say, "A-ha! Our prairie author!" He let her borrow his poetry books, ones he taught from at the college. Uncle Luke said that she was a poet at heart, and would figure it out when the time was right.

There he was now, on a picnic bench. Anna and Laughing Sky weren't far away, but he was alone for a minute. She'd ask him now.

She walked over and sat next to him. "Uncle Luke, I have a question. I'm going to ask everybody but I want to ask you first, because you know both sides of the answer."

He looked at her, "Serious, aren't you?"

"It's important."

He pulled her ponytail gently. "It feels so good right now to be sitting here with you, Iris, you could ask me anything."

Iris looked him in the eye. "What does home mean?"

He was silent. He let her ponytail slip through his fingers. "Iris, I could write a book about that word. Pshew!" He sat still, looked up at his niece, and said, "You took the wind out of my sails. I am home. I left. I came back."

"Were you at home in Bemidji?"

"No. I'm not home anywhere but here. What about you? Are you home?"

Iris looked down at her blue skirt. She smoothed it with her hands. "No." She looked up at her uncle. "Not yet. How long will it take? Uncle Luke, I miss everybody."

"You write them, and they write back, don't they?"

"It's not the same. Not at all. I think I'll ask Mrs Ludvigson. Thanks, Uncle Luke." Iris slid off the bench. She looked back at her uncle and waved. He had a quizzical frown on his face.

Oscar stood right in Iris' path. "Where're you going? You've been busy all day. Now you look like you're going to pick a fight with somebody."

"I'm going to talk to Mrs. Ludvigson. I'm asking people a question."

"Ask me."

"I can't. I don't want to. I'm asking grown-ups."

"Are you saying I'm not grown up? I'm almost grown up. Come on, ask me." Oscar reached out and took one of her hands in his.

Her hand felt small. His had grown.

"If you want the truth, ask me."

"Oscar, you see, I don't want you to be sad."

"Come over here." He led her to steps at the side of the church. "Sit down."

There were no children running around. The activity was at the front of the church. Iris dropped his hand. "Oscar, I want to know what home means. I'm going to ask people until I get the right answer. You don't have to answer if you don't want to."

"Why are you asking this question?"

"I want to know if Harmony will ever feel like home." She

put her elbows on her knees and rested her head in her hands.

"Do your want to go back?"

"Sometimes yes, sometimes, no."

"How about right now? Do you want to leave right now?" Oscar put a hand on her shoulder. It warmed her.

"No, not right now, I guess."

"Good." Oscar sighed.

Iris got up. "Now I'm going to ask Mrs. Ludvigson." Oscar moved his hand. Iris got up and left him there. "Thanks, Oscar."

He hadn't answered her question. He'd asked her some instead. Uncle Luke had too.

Mrs. Ludvigson had taken her hat off and was fanning herself with it. Her auburn hair was up in a knot on the top of her head. Some of it had fallen out and hung in wisps next to her face. She sat in a chair in the shade. At the moment, no one was talking to her. Iris grabbed another chair and pulled it close.

"Well, Iris, I am happy to see you. We are trying to have a happy day in Harmony." She pointed to children Martha Rose's age. They were singing and playing Ring Around the Rosie. Martha Rose was in the middle. "Look at her. Your little sister is getting big."

"I'm glad she's playing. She's real sad about May. Oh, and thank you for teaching her not to say, 'I ain't.'"

"That tragedy went through this town like an electrical shock," answered Mrs. Ludvigson. And, Iris, I know you tried to help Martha Rose with her 'ain'ts'. Sometimes it takes a stranger to make someone listen."

Iris folded her hands in her lap. Sunlight filtered through the trees onto her hands. She looked at her friend. "Mrs. Ludvigson, I've been asking people a question. Then they ask me one back. I want one simple answer. May I ask you?"

"Iris, of course you can. I'll try."

"All right. What does home mean?"

Mrs. Ludvigson looked at her and repeated, "Home?"

"Yes. Home. I'm asking people what does home mean."

Mrs. Ludvigson repeated the word slowly. "H o m e." She looked at Iris and smiled. "Iris, home is where you are loved."

Iris repeated, "Home is where you are loved. Home is where you are loved."

"Yes," said her friend. "Does that help? Oh, I wasn't going to ask you a question!"

"That's the answer! Mrs. Ludvigson, that's the answer! Home is where you are loved. I'm going to tell everyone."

Iris left her friend and found Pastor Nilsen. He was talking to the choir director, Mr. Arcus. Iris waited and waited. At last, Pastor Nilsen saw her standing behind Mr. Arcus. "Iris, do you need something?" he asked.

"Yes, I do. I want to make an announcement."

"An announcement? Some families have left already. Are you sure you want to make an announcement now?"

"I'm sure!" she answered.

Pastor Nilsen nodded to Mr. Arcus. He walked to the top step and clapped his hands. He clapped again, louder. Gradually friends and neighbors stopped talking and turned to him. He stood tall and reached a hand to Iris. "Iris, come here."

Iris walked up and stood next to him. "Iris would like to share something with you. She has," he looked at her, "an announcement."

Iris stood in the afternoon light. How in the world did she get up here in front of these people? What was she thinking?

Pastor Nilsen looked at her.

Iris saw Oscar standing near Mrs. Ludvigson. Her parents looked at her in surprise. Mrs. Vollum had a smile on her face. Uncle Luke had Anna in one arm, and the other around his wife. Then Iris found her voice. She spoke loud and firm. "I have one thing to say. I learned it from Martha Rose's friend. Home is where you are loved." Her face burned. There was silence. She repeated, "Home is where you are loved."

Iris looked at her friends and family. The wind blew the women's skirts in silence. Even the children were still.

Then, her mother grabbed her father. Mrs. Ludvigson hugged Oscar. Pastor Nilsen hugged Iris. Earl Runs Like Fox hugged Laughing Sky. Then he walked over and hugged Mrs. Ludvigson! Mrs. Gonner hugged Julie. Mr. Halker hugged his wife. Mrs. Nielsen hugged Mrs. Halker. Uncle Luke hugged Anna and planted a big kiss on her cheek. May Rhoades's father walked up the steps, shook Pastor Nilsen's hand, and reached for Iris who hugged him hard. Oscar was walking up the steps with his arms out-stretched. Iris looked on as Harmony hugged itself.

It was the first Sunday in August, 1939.